ENTITY

PATRICIA LEEVER

OMNIFIC PUBLISHING
LOS ANGELES

Omnific Publishing
1901 Avenue of the Stars, 2nd floor
Los Angeles, CA 90067
www.omnificpublishing.com

First Omnific eBook edition, November 2014
First Omnific trade paperback edition, November 2014

Library of Congress Cataloguing-in-Publication Data

Leever, Patricia.
    Entity / Patricia Leever – 1st ed.
    ISBN: 978-1-623421-47-2
    1. Supernatural — Romance. 2. Fantasy — Romance.
    3. Demons — Romance. 4. Magic/Occult — Fiction. I. Title

10 9 8 7 6 5 4 3 2 1

Cover Design by Micha Stone and Amy Brokaw
Interior Book Design by Coreen Montagna

Printed in the United States of America

This is for all the women in my life:
my mom, my daughters, sisters-in-law,
nieces, aunts, cousins, and friends.
Every single one of you inspires me to be a better woman,
and I hope that I can do the same for you.
Keep strong, ladies, and remember,
GIRL POWER!

*"The fury of a demon instantly possessed me.
I knew myself no longer. My original soul seemed,
at once, to take its flight from my body;
and a more than fiendish malevolence,
gin-nurtured, thrilled every fibre of my frame."*

~ Edgar Allen Poe, "The Black Cat"

CHAPTER 1
EVELYN

Beep-beep-beep-WHACK!

Honestly, one of these mornings I was going to crack that stupid alarm clock in half trying to hit the snooze button. Damn the morning for rearing its ugly-ass head so friggin' early.

Daniel rolled over, mumbling some semblance of, "Is it time to get up?"

"Uh-huh." I slung my arm over my head and tried to ward the world off for just a minute longer.

"Piss," he complained, stretching beside me like a cat. "Why can't evil take a day off for a change? I don't wanna get up." He flopped his leg over mine and dragged me closer. The feel of his body hair, soft and tickly against me, made me smile at the fact that we were lying here, naked. A giggle bubbled out before I could stop it.

"Damn it," I groaned and gave him a good pinch on his right ass cheek.

"Ow! What was that for?"

"Making me giggle like a girl."

"Well, I hate to break it to ya, babe, but last I checked, you *are* a girl." He flipped up the sheet and stuck his head underneath it. "Yeah, looks like girl parts to me—wait…nope, that's mine." Poking his head back out, he wrapped his arms around me and pulled me in even closer. "One hundred percent, *my* girl."

On mornings like this, I wished to hell I was a "normal" girl. Sometimes I liked to imagine, just for a second, that I was plain old Evelyn with nothing better to do in the morning than lie here with her man.

But that's not how it was. That's not who we were. We were hunters of demons. And when it got down to it, I really wouldn't have had it any other way, because one of the gifts bestowed upon those who hunted was the gift of agelessness. In the real world, I would have shriveled up and kicked the bucket ages ago, not be lying here next to some hot guy one-hundred-plus years my junior.

With a low, bone-melting growl, he nibbled at my neck, and his hands started to wander over my body. His fingers slid across my flesh, up over the curve of my hip, crawling along the outside of my thigh. Rolling my body under his, he trailed kisses over my shoulder as he settled into place, and everything in my being sang to life in anticipation. Man, waking up wrapped in Daniel was possibly one of the best feelings in the world.

When I'd first started out as a hunter it was just me, my mentor and boss Alex, our watcher Isolde, and my handler Tess; but that had been over a hundred years ago when we were living in a little farmhouse just outside of the city. Now, as part of the Lebriga Corporation, we supported five other hunters and their handlers. I wasn't sure how the other branches in the company worked out their living situations, because I'd never lived anywhere other than Los Angeles and bunking with the other female hunters suited me just fine—until Daniel had come along.

This morning was a perfect example of why I was glad we'd talked Alex into letting us have our own room. I mean, we lived in a mansion off of Mulholland now, for Christ's sake; it wasn't like we didn't have the space. Not to mention we weren't the only couple in the house—Josie and Tony had been commandeering the attic as their own personal love nest for ages. Why hadn't they requested this before? It didn't matter, really, because after we'd gotten word from The Powers That Be that the newest visiting hunter, Lana, and her handler, Maria, were going to be a permanent members of the house, I'd known we would have to do something.

There was bad blood between Lana and myself, and I really didn't think I could share a room with her. Yeah, after that assignment a couple of months ago that she helped us out with, she and I had come to an understanding with one another and finally made it to a point where we could almost tolerate each other. But living in the same house with someone and sharing a room were two completely different things.

Beep-beep-beep.

Cursing a blue streak, I reached for the alarm clock, ripped it off the nightstand, and flung it across the room. It made a crunching sound as it smashed against the opposite wall and rained plastic bits onto the floor.

"You're gonna get in trouble for that one of these days. That's what, three in the last month?" Daniel teased as he rolled out of bed, taking the covers with him. He headed toward the bathroom, discarding the sheet in the middle of the room, and turned on the shower. "C'mon, woman, get a move on," he called, sliding the shower curtain open with a whoosh before he stuck his head out of the bathroom door. "We got big bad demons to wrassle, and my back ain't gonna wash itself."

"What if I don't want to wash your back?"

"I'll wash your front," he offered. That lopsided grin of his spread seductively, and his eyes did that sleepy-sexy thing that made me stupid.

I'm never going to be on time for a morning meeting ever again, am I?

Nope.

Will it be worth it?

Daniel waggled his eyebrows and his tongue at me.

Hells yeah!

I leaped out of the bed and raced across the room, practically tackling Daniel in the shower.

We were only twenty minutes late to the morning meeting, but we got a good dose of stink-eye from Alex and a muttered something about either "humping and bunnies" or "monkeys from Z."

Lately, the meetings had been virtually the same anyway. Three bodies had been found in three weeks, literally turned inside out and missing every single internal organ, with every bone cracked open and the marrow sucked clean. As a matter of fact, the only things that had been left of these women were hollowed out bones and empty sacks of skin. That screamed Chilgaz demon, without a doubt.

Luckily, none of the information had been released to the public, but according to our source inside the LAPD, that was going to change soon. The chief of police was prepping for a press conference regarding the murders, and that was precisely what we didn't need. Part of our job as hunters was keeping the public unaware of the more horrific demon habits—the things that lurked in dark corners, waiting to make your frightening nightmares a reality. That's what we went after, taking care of the problem before humankind even knew about it.

Our first plan of attack was Josie, our resident supermodel. At nearly six feet tall, with long blond hair and legs that didn't quit, she was our go-to gal for catching the creeper demon types. Men of every species—hell, most females too, if we're being honest—wanted to rub themselves all over Josie every chance they got. But as great as Jo was for luring in anything with half a brain and a sliver of a sex drive, subtlety wasn't exactly her strong suit. She'd gone after this guy with everything she had, tits a-blazing and wearing a skirt so damned short *I* could damn near see up the thing. But apparently this Chilgaz wasn't one for aggressive prey. Josie had slid up into one of the clubs he'd been spotted in and was propositioned by everything in the joint *except* him. She might as well have been a leper for all the attention he'd paid her.

It really sucked when a plan didn't go the way we wanted it to, which, for as kick-ass at our jobs as we were, was more often than not. Back at the drawing board, there was a brief discussion about sending our new hunter Lana in. Hailing from the Ukraine, she was a stone-cold killer and the closest thing Lebriga had to an actual ninja. She could sneak into a joint and dispense of a demon with such precision it made the hair on the back of *my* neck stand on end. No muss, no fuss; slice and dice the fucker and be home for dinner. When it came to luring anything in, however, she tended to favor Jo's brand of mantrapping.

Case in point: When she'd first met Daniel, she had shoved her tongue down his throat as a means of greeting. Granted, he and I hadn't hooked up yet, but it was still a sore spot with me, despite burying the proverbial hatchet between us. It was a moot point anyway, though, since that method had proven ineffective in this case. And as fabulous as it would've been to just have her whoosh in and make sushi out of this guy, we needed to get to his lair to make sure he was working alone and not keeping any innocents on hand for later snackage.

The window we had before the story broke to the public was closing fast, and we needed to get this joker yesterday.

So I was up to bat, working my no-one-loves-me-lonely-girl best. I was seriously beginning to wonder if I should be honored or offended that I always wound up playing that role.

Honored.

Mostly because one of the best parts of my job as a hunter was getting the drop on a demon that thought he'd scored an easy mark. That look on their faces when I revealed myself was what all those "priceless" commercials were all about.

Itchy wig: Three-day scalp irritation.

Age spell: Occasional residual acne.

The look on the scumbag's face when I whipped off the wig and pulled my Divinity blade off of my back: Priceless!

It was almost as good as watching the life in their eyes fade to black as I sent them back to Hell, or whatever nasty world they'd crawled out of. Yeah, definitely honored.

Donning my frumpy best, I lurked in every back-alley club in the area where the bodies had been found for an entire week before we got a hit. It was about frickin' time, too; my temples were pounding with every bass beat of that damned music they seemed to play in all of these places. I'd begun to think that they played the same song in every hellhole of a joint, and if I had to sit through another night of listening to this poor excuse for "music," I would have to strangle one of those deejays with their own ridiculously stupid headphones.

A millisecond before my last nerve completely snapped in half, Mr. Demonlicious strolled through the club door like he owned the joint. This guy really thought he was something on a stick, working some kind of Eurotrash vibe as he waltzed in, fist-bumped the bartender and deejay, and proceeded to scan the crowd. I guess he wouldn't be bad looking, if you were horribly desperate and liked that sort of thing. Or if I weren't a hunter and couldn't see the foul being sliding around under his guise of human flesh—the sick twist of creature that would send men and women screaming into the night if they knew what was walking next to them. Yeah, I supposed the vaguely European accent, slicked back hair, and suave, devil-may-care swagger might be appealing to the average human chick, especially one who had a low opinion of herself.

Now if I could just get him to look in my direction. Damn, he seemed to be checking out every chick in the place *but* me.

This was going to be a pain in my ass.

Straightening my back a touch, I tossed my hair over my shoulder, swirled my straw around in my drink, and casually looked up from under my lashes in his general direction. He hadn't moved far, and now he wasn't alone. The girl he stood next to looked like she might have been pretty if she tried but had given up and resigned herself to thick glasses, bad skin, and probably self-esteem so low you'd have to dig a trough just to get to it. Talking to her, he leaned closer and closer until he toyed with a lock of her hair. He'd found what he was looking for and was marking his prey, making sure, in no uncertain circumstances, that this was his. Chilgaz didn't like to share their meals, even with their own kind. They took their feeding seriously as an intimate act between the consumer and the consumed. This was no longer a sting operation but a search-and-recover gig. Not optimal but definitely doable.

A waitress dropped off a fresh drink at the table, and he slid the glass to his victim, encouraging her to imbibe, which made my gut twist into knots. When I had noticed the girl before, I'd taken an initial scan of the place, and she'd been halfway to drunk even then. I'd also noted that she'd sucked down two umbrella-laden glasses of something blue since. Now add whatever that green stuff was in this last glass and she'd likely agree to anything he suggested, which was what he wanted, I was sure. After the girl had finished off her final drink, the demon bowed elegantly, offered her a hand like he was Prince Charming or some shit, and they were up and quietly slipping out the back door.

This was it.

"Be advised, plan B is in effect. Elvis is leaving the building and I'm in pursuit," I muttered, throwing some money down for my drink and making a beeline after them.

"Ten-four, Big Ev. Danny Boy and I will be right on your six," Tony assured. I knew he would be, too. Tony was *that* guy. The one who made smart-ass comments and inappropriate jokes about boobs and farts and gave everyone nicknames so cheesy you couldn't help but roll your eyes and shake your head. But for all of that, you could count on him to have your back out in the field, one hundred percent of the time.

I snuck out into the back alley and followed the demon and the girl for two blocks before he led her into a converted warehouse, the type of dwelling the Chilgaz demons favored because it had plenty of space to store their leavings. Most demons that consumed humans worked that way. They preferred to suck every ounce of nutrition they could out of their human feed and hide what was left of the body so no one would be the wiser. Quiet and clean.

Not all demons used humans for food, though. While most did, there were some that would just as soon eat a tire as put their lips on human flesh. Those typically used humans for breeding, slavery, or some kind of twisted entertainment that usually involved torture.

Yeah, there were the real sickos that got off on leaving a mess, but we weren't dealing with a psycho looking to bring attention to himself by leaving bodies behind. This was someone that got sloppy for a different purpose. The bodies we'd found weren't displayed as a trophy but discarded like chicken bones. This was a feeding frenzy by a demon so food-drunk that it just left its table full of carnage for someone else to clean up because it just didn't care.

Daniel and Tony caught up with me out front, and we tiptoed along the side of the warehouse and behind the building to the back door.

"What's the skinny, Ev?" Tony asked.

"He's in there with a woman, brown hair, early twenties. I'm betting this place is pretty big on the inside, so we need to get the hell in there, split up, and find this bastard before it's too late. I'll take point," I advised.

"You're in charge, boss," Daniel replied with a wink.

"Only in the field, baby."

"That's disgusting," Tony said as he picked the lock. "I'm trying to work here, you guys. Quit being gross."

Daniel smirked and handed me my wrapped Divinity blade, the silver handle of his own sword winking at me over his shoulder in the moonlight. I always felt more comfortable going into a fight with my blade in my hands. She was a deadly weapon in her own right, but with one drop of my blood, she sang to life with ancient magic. A Divinity blade was created for a hunter before he or she was even born, locked up tight until the hunter was ready to wield the powerful brand of magic imbued in the very metal. No two blades were the same. Bonded to its hunter by blood, the steel shocked any other creature to near death. It was an honor that not every hunter was allowed and one we took very seriously. I slid the leather straps of the holster over my shoulders and made sure she was on tight.

Tony soon sprang the latch with a soft click and pushed the heavy metal door open without even a creak. Stealing through the back of the warehouse, we made our way across the concrete floor. Hooks hung from the ceiling in rows and tiers. The entire room was littered with band and table saws. This must have been a meatpacking plant once. Everything seemed clean; no blood or debris was visible, but there was a stench. A very distinct odor that one just never got used to. Death. More specifically, decay. Passing over one of the drains in the floor, I saw clumps of blond hair strung around the grate.

As we reached the back of the room, we opened the door there and were immediately hit with an overwhelming floral scent. Clearly it was meant to mask the smell of death, but the mixture of the two was downright nauseating.

The sound of soft music coming from someplace deep inside the building led us to a room illuminated by a sea of candles. A trail of them also lit the way down a corridor. A bit of ambiance for his prey. Typical Chilgaz behavior. He would let her believe she was living out her ultimate handsome-man "fantasy" with him. Little did she know that the road only led to one place…a horrific and excruciating death.

Silently motioning to Daniel and Tony, I made my way down the hall with them. I pulled my blade out of the sheath, the weight of the metal feeling good in my hands.

The music grew louder as we moved closer, and we began to hear a soft-accented murmur. The demon was casting his spell on the poor girl, weaving his macabre web of deceit around her. He practically purred as he praised her unconventional beauty, promised her untold riches, and proclaimed his undying love for her. His dulcet voice painted pictures of paradise and carved out a life for them that would never happen, anything and everything she could possibly want to hear until she was all but putty in his ravenous claws, swaying mindlessly with him.

We poked our heads around the corner to get a visual on the situation — that was practically protocol rule one. If all was copasetic, we would strike as planned: jump in, off the demon, escort the girl out to the cleanup crew, and sweep the rest of the warehouse for more victims or any other demons that might lurk about.

Apparently not all was hunky dory, though, as Daniel gave the signal to fall back. We retreated into the floral room.

"There better be a Goddamned good reason why you pulled us out of there." I tried not to sound irritated, but the need to finish the hunt was tinting my voice with frustration. It was part of our hunter genetics; when we were around demons, we had a nearly uncontrollable urge to gut them. Suppressing that need, in any way, put us on edge. I knew Daniel understood this by the look on his face and the tension in his stance.

"I know her," he hissed.

"What do you mean, you know her?" Tony asked. "Didn't Gabriel recruit you and Chris out of somewhere in the Midwest or some shit? Why the hell do they call it 'Midwest' anyway? I mean, I get the 'mid' part, but it's not exactly west, maybe mid-north —"

"Seriously?" I growled before turning back to Daniel. "How do you know her? Do you think she'd recognize you?"

"I don't know if she's vacationing or moved here, but my family lived across the street from hers. I've known her my whole life."

"Shit." I pushed a hand through my hair as I formulated a new plan of action. "Okay, this is what needs to happen: Daniel, you sweep the rest of the warehouse. Chilgaz typically work alone, so I don't think you'll find anything, but that will get you away from the girl because —"

"Meagan," he said.

"What?"

"Her name is Meagan."

I stared at Daniel for a second, letting my mind wrap around the fact that he knew her. She was a real person that he'd had a relationship with. It didn't matter what the basis of that relationship was; there was clearly something. I shook my head to clear it — now was not the time for a jealous-girlfriend moment.

"Sorry," I continued. "Meagan cannot see you. I'll distract the demon, and, Tony, I want you to get her the hell out of here. Clear?"

"Clear," they said in unison.

Daniel broke off to check the remainder of the warehouse while Tony and I moved back down the hall and entered the room. The Chilgaz loomed over Meagan. One arm twined around her body, poised to take hold of her and steady her in place. The other hand crept around her head, fingers sliding through her hair to take a firm grip as he tilted her face up to his. A thin shaft with rows of teeth protruded from his mouth, ready to enter hers and begin its descent into her gullet.

Why wasn't she screaming or trying to pull away?

He moved their bodies to the music, turning her just enough for me to see that she had her eyes shut and lips pursed, ready to receive the demon's deadly kiss.

Chicken-shit asshole wouldn't even give her the opportunity to fight back. I wasn't going to let that happen.

I cleared my throat loudly, and the demon froze. When his eyes flicked up to mine, our gazes locked. He twirled Meagan out of his arms and sat her on a nearby crate. His moves were so fluid and graceful that I barely noticed he'd slurped his tongue back into his mouth and was headed in my direction with his damn hypnotic blue eyes putting me in a near trance. Hell, I'd bet this dude had even taken down his fair share of hunters in his time because he was just that good.

But I was better.

"Welcome," he crooned as he slid closer. His focus was so fixed on me that he didn't notice Tony slip around behind him to scoop the girl off the crate and carry her out to safety. "I am Isiel, and how may I address this beautiful creature before me?"

That was a new one. In all the years I'd been doing this, not one single demon asked what my name was. I honestly didn't know if I should lie or be straight with him.

"Um, Evelyn...I guess."

"Evelyn," he repeated, drawing out every syllable as if he could taste the sound. His eyes bore into mine, the ice-blue irises twisting, turning lazily, trying to worm their way into my head. "Darling Evelyn, we are civilized people, aren't we? Why don't you put that nasty sword away so we can have a proper chat?"

I could feel the vibration of his voice slithering over my skin. That's how these guys worked, using their voices, spinning eyes, and human good looks to lull their victims into relaxing.

Good thing Tony was aces when it came to technology. He'd custom fit us all with noise-canceling ear protection tuned to the frequency of the Chilgaz's sound waves and contact lenses that filtered out the twirling eyes' effects. Better yet, the demon didn't know any of that, and I kinda liked to keep it that way.

I wanted him to get in a little bit closer so I could get a clean shot. So, playing the stupefied prey, I nodded and slid my sword back into the scabbard on my back. I really didn't want to use it on him anyway; a .45 to the head would be much cleaner.

"Very good," he purred, moving in right next to me, his finger brushing against my cheek, over my shoulder, and down to my hand. With a quick flick of his wrist, he twirled me around and lowered me into one of those fancy dips they do on that dance show. "You know, Evelyn, I did see you in the club. Do you know that? I saw you trying to be demure, quiet, like a little mouse sneaking around the cat's domain. But what you did not know is that I am not your ordinary cat."

Another jerk of movement had me back on my feet and wrapped in his arms, the hot humidity of his breath slithering over the shell of my ear as he continued his attempt to lull me into submission.

"I can smell a hunter, even through all those silly charms and potions you try to cover yourself with. You all have a distinct stench about you that normally isn't very pleasant, but you, Evelyn, do you know what you smell like to me, right now, trembling in my arms?"

"No," I whispered.

"Ambrosia," he hummed as he took a deep breath. "Ahhh, I don't know how you smell this way. Part of me wants to keep you with me just so I can breathe in your decadent aroma every day. But the other part of me cannot wait to sink into your mouth and lose myself in what is sure to be the most divine meal I will ever have."

He spun me to face him and looked me up and down. His tongue peeked from between his lips as he breathed heavily out of his open mouth. He looked like he was about to jizz right there, and I tried not to recoil at the thought — not to mention his rancid demon breath was seriously foul.

"Ask me to kiss you," he said, panting.

Fighting the bile rising in my throat, I leaned in toward his ear and whispered, "Isiel, kiss…mmmy ass."

"What?" His voice cracked and his head jerked back, complete and utter shock written all over his face. "I-I don't understand."

"Aw c'mon, dude, seriously? You just told me that you knew I was a hunter. What else did you expect? I've been watching you for the better part of a week. You're not *that* dumb."

His nostrils flared and his head tilted unnaturally as he took a few steps back, I assumed, to make a run for it.

But everyone knows what happens when you assume things.

"Are you mocking me?" His lip twitched. "That's not very ladylike."

"Yeah, that whole 'lady' thing was never my strong suit. I've always been more of a fuck-it-and-see-what-happens kind of gal."

"You are absolutely vulgar," he spat, his chest rising and falling rapidly with each word. "I shall enjoy shredding your larynx even more on my way to your filthy hunter gullet!" With lightning speed he launched himself, barbed tongue whipping in the air like some slimy weapon.

I dropped to the floor, but his serpentine tongue caught on my cheek and sliced it to the bone as he sailed over my head and crashed into a stack of candles. Chilgaz saliva was extremely acidic and liquefied all the organs and soft tissue inside the body. That was how they could slurp out so much of their victims. Luckily for me, it took a while for their acid to work its way through bone, but it stung like a son of a bitch; there was no way around that. I knew I had to get treated soon if I wanted to keep my face.

Isiel picked himself up off the floor and hissed at me.

"I seriously hope that is candle wax on your pants and not some 'premature' accident, 'cause I know you were getting a little too excited back there, and yeah, that's pretty gross. Have some self-control."

The demon roared and flew at me again, slashing with claws that now protruded out of his fingertips, ones that he used to hold his prey as he devoured them alive. I ducked the attack and reached for my gun. My face was really starting to hurt, and I just wanted to end this guy. Out of the corner of my eye, I saw Daniel enter the room.

His eyes locked on the bubbling wound on my cheek, and I watched as his focus shifted, fixating on the demon across from me. I could practically see the wheels turning in his head and knew what was about to happen. Daniel was already amped up because he knew the girl this guy had been ready to have for dinner, and now I had a nice gash on my face thanks to our little friend over there. I knew what I would do if the roles were reversed.

This demon dude was toast.

Daniel's Divinity blade was off of his back, slicing his palm, and singing though the air before you could blink. The room was alight with his glow as his blood made contact with the sword, springing the weapon to life.

I had to admit, the beauty of it took me aback. No doubt the image of a hot guy with an average, everyday sword was tasty as all get-out, but the sight of Daniel with an ancient mystical weapon like the Divinity blade, fully activated, locked and loaded and ready for battle? Yeah, there was no possible way anything in this world or the next was as magical and magnificent as that.

I caught my breath when I heard the blade tear through the demon's flesh. Daniel attacked with such force that he drove Isiel back five feet to the wall, pinning him between the sword and brick. Blood and hormones raced through my veins when Daniel whispered, "With my sword I damn you and send you back to Hell..." The distinct scrape of metal being pulled from stone and the sucking sound of Daniel's blade leaving Isiel's stomach made my entire body quiver.

Shit if that wasn't as sexy as hell.

"Meagan's safe with the cleanup crew. They're taking extra care of her as Daniel's friend. She won't remember a thing about tonight," Tony said as he strolled back into the room. "Damn, did I miss it? Who stuck the big bad guy in the gut with a big bad sword? Was it you or Danny Boy?"

"He did." I nodded to Daniel, feeling an overwhelming sense of pride in that moment. Not only for being the one who had trained Daniel to his current level of excellence, but because he was mine.

All mine.

CHAPTER 2
DANIEL

Holy hell.

Evie and I had barely made it back to the house after making short work of that Chilgaz asswipe when she yanked me upstairs, shoved me into our room, and leapt on me like a cheetah.

Not that I was complaining. Right now we were half hanging off the bed, panting like we'd just sprinted our way through a 26k marathon. She was sprawled on top of me, spent as all hell. God I loved after-assignment sex.

I navigated my way through the mass of her hair that was flopped over my face and found the mark on her cheek. It was healing already, thanks to the magic goop our healer Isolde had cooked up and slathered on her. The bone wasn't exposed anymore, but there was a significant pink divot where it *had* been.

The fight suddenly came back to me. When I had walked back into the room at the warehouse and seen that wound on Evie's face, the shocking white of her cheekbone peeking through the blood, my vision shrank to the creature that had dared lay a finger—or a tongue, as it were—on her. The filth that had tried to do the same to Meagan. All I could think about was ending him, right then and there. Sure, I knew Evie wasn't some shrinking violet who needed a man to come in and vanquish the bad guys for her. Far from it. Shoot, she could wipe the floor with my ass on an off day, and I was man enough to admit that. But that didn't stop the primitive urge in me to protect her.

I clenched my teeth against the rage as I raised a hand to her face and ran a thumb under the mark on her cheek. She turned her face away from my touch.

"Shit, babe, I'm sorry. Does it hurt? If it still does, you should go back to see Isolde."

"No," she answered immediately—too immediately, if you asked me, which probably meant it was still sore but she was too freaking stubborn to admit it. "I mean, it did, when it happened, but it's fine now."

I knew damned well she wasn't being completely honest with me, but I also knew if I pushed the issue she'd fight me on it. And I didn't want to fight. Not right now, not with her, anyway. Taking her face in my hands, I gently pulled her down to lay soft kisses across the scar. A sigh poured out of her, and I smiled as I continued across her face. I knew her; I knew exactly what little moves made her bones turn to jelly, and I loved the feeling of her body melting against mine.

"I've been doing this for over a hundred years," she said, "and I'm not gonna lie, I've had to have my ass saved on more than one occasion. But when you do it, I don't know. It opens up something primal in me and makes me completely insane. I want to claw all your clothes off and get as close to you as I possibly can right in the middle of God and everybody, and it takes everything in me to wait until we're alone."

I felt her hand slide down my body and over my hip and caught my breath when she found what she was looking for. Damn, she sure knew how to stroke more than my ego.

"Baby, I'll save your ass any day of the week and twice on Sunday if this is how you say thank you." I rolled her underneath me.

The next few weeks, things plugged along. Catch a demon, kill a demon. Everything was pretty normal on the surface—normal for us, anyway. Only, something seemed…off.

At first I thought it was just me being thrown off from my near encounter with Meagan. It had been such a shock to see her. To my family and the rest of the outside world, Daniel Summers had died, and over the last couple years that I'd been a hunter, I'd had to forget most of my old life. It was a survival mechanism, if you wanted to put a label on it. We all did it. You had to in this line of work because you were going to outlive anyone you'd ever known. I'd be lying if I said I didn't think about my mom and dad from time to time and what this must have done to them. But I had to look at the bigger picture, the work that I was doing now.

Shit, what *was* I doing now?

I was staring at the ceiling of the training room with Evie sitting on my chest and her forearm pressed to my throat.

"What the hell?" She sat back, panting. "If I was a demon you'd be dead right now. You can't check out like that, Daniel, not even for a second."

"Sorry," I said with a sigh as I sat up. Evie slid down my stomach and into my lap, and my arms went around her almost out of instinct. I kissed her shoulder before I laid my chin on it. "I'm just…I don't know, ever since—"

Evie huffed, pulled out of my arms, and bounded to her feet. "There's no excuse for dropping your guard. You drop your guard out in the field and you'll be dead. Period. Now get your ass up and get ready to go again."

"What the hell is your problem?" I asked as I got to my feet.

She answered in typical Evie fashion, a running shoulder to the gut that lifted me off the ground a good two feet. Okay, so this was how she wanted to play it.

As soon as I landed, I gripped her around the middle, popped her off of the ground, and prepared to pile drive her. But before I could lower the boom, she whipped her legs around my neck and squeezed. The shift threw me off balance, and I fell backward with Evie's thighs wrapped around my head. Struggling to stay conscious, I picked up my feet and used the momentum to catapult my torso up, effectively bending her in half. She didn't let go, but it loosened her grip enough for me to breathe.

"Babe, normally I love being trapped between your thighs, but I have feeling you're not in the mood."

Her thighs clenched for a second or twenty before she released me and clocked me in the jaw with her heel. As she rolled away, I grabbed her right foot to jerk her off balance, and she landed on her back with a thud.

"What is your problem?" I asked again as I stood and held out a hand to help her to her feet.

"My problem is that my trainee isn't taking this seriously." She snatched my hand, planted a foot in my chest, and launched me across the training room, ass end over teacup. I lay there for a minute, waiting for her to get close enough, and when she did, I swept her legs out from under her and pinned her to the ground.

She struggled underneath me, but I knew that if she really wanted to get loose, she could, even though I outweighed her by over a hundred pounds. But she didn't; she just glared up at me, jaw clenched tight, nostrils flared. I'd never seen her this pissed off, not even when she'd hated me.

"This isn't foreplay, Daniel," she barked.

"Since when?"

"Since…" Evie closed her eyes and shook her head. "Never mind, it's stupid. Just let me up, please."

I moved to the side and she sat up. When she went to stand, I put my hand on her arm to stop her.

"Look, I don't know what I did to tick you off, but clearly I've done something. You're jumping all over my ass for not being focused when the only thing you're focused on is pounding my ass into the ground, and I have no idea why." But by the time I'd gotten to the end of my little diatribe, I was feeling pretty agitated myself, more so than I normally would be.

"You. Didn't. Do. Anything." She bit off each word as her hands curled into fists and she punched the mat beneath us so hard the whole floor shook. "It's me. Shit that is running around in my own head, okay, and I don't know any other way to deal with it."

"Uh, you can try talking to me instead of trying to bash my head in." I scooted closer to her and tilted her chin up to look into her eyes; unshed tears shimmered around their edges.

"Do you miss your old life?" she asked quietly. "You're still new at this. The real world is still fresh in your memory, and after seeing that girl in the warehouse, the one you knew…" She shrugged her shoulders, "I don't know. Like I said, it's stupid."

"It's not stupid," I assured her, pulling her into my arms. "I'll be honest, seeing Meagan did stir up memories of what I was before I came here." I felt her stiffen against me.

"Did you love her?"

"What? No." I chuckled, trying to play it off as nothing, but the sound was tight and had a bitter edge to it. "We had a thing a long time ago, but seeing her made me think of my family, my parents."

"That's understandable." She wrapped her arms around my middle and took a deep breath. "I've been feeling so weird lately, like…"

"Something bad is about to happen?"

"Exactly."

Evie's and my suspicions explained a lot. Everyone in the house seemed to be running hot. It was almost as if all the hunters in the house could feel the evil swirling and building in the air, and I didn't like it in the slightest. It put us all on edge.

Our natural hunter instinct was kicking in, our sixth sense of sorts. We could feel anything sinister brewing before it had a chance to bubble over into the world. It made the little hairs on the back of our necks stand on end and butterflies take flight in our stomachs. Our skin practically itched in anticipation when something really big was cooking, and sure as shit, everyone was practically coming undone.

In contrast, I noticed that all of the handlers had gone oddly quiet. It made sense, really. Hunters and handlers were a team, and what good was a team if both parts of it went batshit? Hunters acted; we were the ones who went out and got our hands dirty killing demons. Handlers, though, they were like the inside guy — the ones who knew the whos, the whys, and the wheres. Their job was to make *our* job run as smoothly as possible. Every hunter was paired with one. Bonded, actually, two halves of a whole. It was the only logical explanation for the handlers' complete stoicism.

Holy shit, this was going to be really bad.

The following day, our hunter's meeting ran like clockwork, which was surprising because lately you had to slice your way through all the tension to get to your seat. I should have known that was the first sign this was all about to come to a head.

Alex, resident boss man, ran the show. He had the direct line to Corporate; everything went through him — every assignment, every new bit of intel to follow, probably every time we all took a shit. His job was to manage, as he knew everyone's abilities and handicaps, knew who could do what, how fast, and with the least amount of collateral damage to the human world. Not that he was just a desk jockey. Not even close. He could walk the walk and talk the talk, and when he said jump, the only acceptable answers from us were which direction and how high.

"Good morning," he began. "Today, as much as I'd like to proceed with our usual agenda, another order of business has landed in our backyard, so to speak. You've all felt the *change in air*, as it were. If you recall, the last time the hunters of the house were in this state of vexation was shortly before we tangled with Mzetir."

Everyone sucked in a breath. Mzetir, leader of the Aremoc clan, was one nasty motherfucker. Not only had he tried to take over the world, but he'd tried doing it with demon hybrids, and the asshole wanted to use my girlfriend as his baby mama. It had taken the entire team of hunters, including Alex and our handlers, to take down that son of a bitch. That was some hairy-ass shit, man.

"I'm glad you all remember, because this might just be worse." With a nod to his left, Alex gave the floor to Lana, the newest member of the house and a psychic.

She stood beside Alex, looking exceedingly uneasy. Oh man, she'd seen something, something worse than Mzetir. What the hell could be worse than that guy?

"All of my life I have had a certain vision, one that I could never get a hold of completely. It is much like a flame, flickering inside of my mind, wavering on a breeze and going out just as fast. Over the years I have tried to capture it, working my mind, stretching it as far as I could to try to grasp something." She stopped for a moment, wiping her palms on her jeans as she shifted back and forth on her feet. "When the vision comes, it plagues me for a month or two. Once, it stayed for an entire year and nearly drove me insane. Three weeks ago, the visions began again." Lana looked to Isolde. "Thankfully, I had Isolde to guide me this time. I went to her, and together we were able to harness a more complete picture of the demon inside my mind…a Spectoral."

"That makes complete sense," Z muttered. "Those Specs are slippery bastards." Z was our demon guy. If it slithered, had horns, or spewed slime from its eyeballs, he knew what it was and, better yet, the best way to kill it. And kill it he could, man. Homeboy was at least six-five if he was a foot and as wide as a fridge. I wanted to not like the guy because he'd had a thing with Evie back in the day, but the truth was, that was in the past and he was good people.

"Not to sound like a complete rookie here, but uh, what's a Spectoral?" I asked.

"A Spectoral demon is a nasty one, and quite wily, as Zachary pointed out," Alex explained. It was funny how he called us all by our full names, like the linguistic part of him had refused to evolve over the years. "They have no physical body, therefore they must inhabit a host of sorts, preferably humans. When they enter into the physical body of a human, they bind themselves to the soul, taking over everything about that individual. Some *possessions*, if you will, happen at a very young age, unfortunately, but theoretically it could happen at any point in a human's life. These demons liken themselves to gods. They crave the power of having followers to do their bidding. Some of the more notable Spectorals have caused quite a ruckus in the human world: Jim Jones, David Koresh, and of course Charles Manson. As you would imagine, Spectorals are notoriously cult leaders.

"Over the years, the main office has observed a presence. This entity has presented itself in several different venues, lingering just long enough for us to catch a trail before it vanishes, only to resurface in a year or so elsewhere."

"Sounds like Anabael," Z said, straightening in his chair. Of course he would know who it was. Being our resident demon expert, he had his finger on the pulse of everything that happened in the demon realm. He had informants in every clan and corner of every level of Hell and otherworldly dimension. "She's one cagy-ass bitch from what I've seen, and as far as I know, she's the only one that moves like that."

"Precisely," Alex confirmed with a nod. "She favors the more subtle approach, heading up companies that lure humans using one of their greatest weaknesses: money. You'll find her behind some of the biggest consultant-driven organizations, raising them to near cult status before she moves on to a new venture. Corporate has discovered that her newest business enterprise is one you may have heard of. She is calling herself Annabelle Simmons, founder of Beautiful Illuminations."

That name did sound familiar. I seemed to recall a late-night TV session with Evie when we'd caught an infomercial starring a gaggle of girls explaining how they had all this extra money to buy clothes and crap because they'd started selling some junk they slathered on their face. If I remembered correctly, the big draw was that you could get "Paid to Party," which seemed to make them all squeal. Yeah, that had to be it. I distinctly remembered Evie saying something about holding back the urge to barf.

"Is that the one that's supposed to be empowering for young women?" Evie asked. "Something like 'made by women for women' and 'be your own woman while you're young' and 'take what you want from life' or some shit like that?"

"That is the very one. And I'm pleased to see you know so much about the company already, Evelyn," he said with *that* look. Alex always wore a serious face, but he did this thing with his eyebrows that made them all pinchy, and you just knew he was about to tell you something you didn't want to hear.

"You might as well just lay it out on the table," Evie said. That was my girl; she didn't mince words or beat around the bush, not even with Alex. "What am I not going to like about this assignment, Alex?"

Taking a deep breath, he sat back in his chair and did that tent thing with his fingers. Man alive, that was the other thing he did when shit was about to get real. Damn, this was going to be bad.

"Corporate has run several different scenarios through their own psychics, and at present, the only plan of attack is to get you into their headquarters…alone."

That flipped my *oh-shit* switch. I jumped out of my seat so fast my chair toppled over, prepared to protest this insanity. Christ, if this was half as bad as he was making it out to be without even knowing dick about what was even happening, he sure as shit wasn't sending her in alone. Not if I had anything to say about it. Fuck that noise. My mouth opened up, and I was about ready to give my boss the tongue lashing of his life, but before I could pop off a single word, Alex raised a palm in my direction.

"If I could finish?" he asked, with a discerning cock of his eyebrow.

My mouth automatically closed as I slowly picked up my chair and sat back down. I gritted my teeth and could feel my nostrils flare as I breathed to keep my calm.

"Thank you," he said to me before he turned back to Evie. "As I was saying, for the most part, you will be alone. However, I've been assured that you will have a support system watching your every move. Gabriel is coming to discuss the details later this afternoon. He wants to speak with you himself, Evelyn."

That, in a nutshell, ended the meeting, but I continued to fume over it all. Being relatively new to the hunter business, I still struggled with certain things. Keeping my temper and my mouth shut when being given orders were two of them. Not that Evie was one to talk. She had a lot of hunting years on me, and more often than not, she popped off with her opinion of a situation—especially if it was something that would put anyone but her in the line of fire.

We ended up in the training ring again, going rounds with each other and trying to blow off some steam, but nothing seemed to lighten my mood. I was livid.

"Relax," she said. "I was alone when we took off after that Chilgaz demon a few weeks ago, and I was fine. You and Tony had my back, and we all came out—"

"Fine?" I eyeballed the spot on her cheek that had been sliced open. "If you'll recall, you almost had your face sucked off. I wouldn't exactly call that fine, Evelyn."

"Yeah, and over the course of a century, I've almost been eaten, almost stabbed, almost turned into goo…you want me to go on? I was hunting before your grandparents were zygotes, and if you'll notice, there is a pattern here: *almost*. I'm not a delicate little flower, babe. I can take care of myself."

No, she wasn't a delicate little flower. She was a cactus. A prickly, hard-as-fuck-to-kill, stab-me-in-the-ass-when-I'm-not-looking cactus. But she was *my* cactus, damn it, and I cared about her more than I cared about any other creature on this planet.

"What if this time it isn't 'almost'?" Pacing to the wall, I hit my head and fists against it, my teeth clenching together. "The 'not almost' only happens once, Ev."

Her arms circled my waist, and I felt her weight as she laid her cheek against my back.

"I know," she said quietly, planting a soft kiss on my spine. I loved the way her skin felt against mine. "But this is the job, Daniel. You know that."

Every one of my muscles tensed and released. Yeah, I knew that this was the job. I had known going in that I would be asked to do things for the greater good that might make me feel uncomfortable. I'd known I'd have to follow orders and that those orders had a purpose, even if I didn't understand them.

But I hadn't known about her. I hadn't known I would find the love of my life in a hard-headed, foul-mouthed, pain in my ass. I hadn't known she would be the one thing in this world that I absolutely could not live without.

Placing my hand over hers, I gave it a squeeze. "I just wish someone would have told me that this part of it, the part where I have to sit back and watch while you go off to hunt, was going to suck so much."

"Would it have made a difference? Honestly?"

I whirled around and took her face in my hands, staring down at her. Her eyes always transfixed me. I felt like I could see my entire world in the different shades of blue and flecks of green and gold. I looked over every inch of her face, rubbing one thumb along her full bottom lip and where the scar on her cheek had been weeks ago. This was a trick question.

"No, damn it, not one freaking iota. If Gabriel would have walked into my dorm room that day and told me straight up that I was going to meet my slice of heaven in one little bitty brown-haired, blue-eyed girl and she was going to carry my heart out there into the field every time she stepped out the door, I wouldn't have believed it was possible. But all it would have taken was one second in the room with you and I'd sell my soul to the devil if they'd asked me to."

"God, don't say that." She gave me a slap on the chest. "Don't even joke about that. Luce is an ass and would probably find a way to sneak a contract to you if he thought he had half a chance."

"Wait…Luce? As in short for Lucifer? You have a nickname for the freaking devil?"

"Yes, the very one, and he's a complete douchebag."

I had to shake my head. *Wait a minute…*

"Look, it was a long time ago and I was new," she said. "I kind of, almost, slept with him. Luckily Alex found me before anything could happen."

"What? How?"

"He can be very charming and flattering. He's really pretty when he looks human, okay? Just ask Tony and Z. He's...he's not gender specific. Actually, I'm surprised he didn't pop in to see you before you signed up with Lebriga. Maybe he's waiting for the right time. If I were you, I'd keep your eyes peeled, and don't drop the soap in the shower when you're alone."

Was she serious? My mouth dropped open and closed. Open and closed. I probably looked like a fish, but words wouldn't form. What do you say to that?

"Breathe, I'm kidding," she assured me through bouts of laughter. "Well, mostly. Yes, I've met him, yes, he's a douche, but no I've never almost slept with him. However, he is really, *really* pretty. That's the God's honest truth, as much as I hate to admit it."

That little shit. She loved to tweak my nose every chance she got. And I loved her for it. I also loved to get her back for it. Narrowing my eyes at her, I honed in on her one weakness. With lightning fast fingers, I attacked her secret tickle spot. Before she could escape my clutches, she was on the floor, gasping for air and curled in a ball, probably trying not to piss all over herself.

My tickle assault didn't last very long, though; it ended almost as soon as she hit the floor, when my bone-deep need to hold her took over. I pulled her in close and held her tight, wrapping my body around hers as we lay on the padded training room floor. Her breathing returned to normal, the laughter subsiding, and I burrowed my face into the back of her neck, my lips pressing against the Eye of Serendipity tattoo, drinking in the strength that it gave off for me.

It was funny how that worked. The tattoo's charmed ink always seemed to know what I needed and how to give it to me without taking away from Evie's own needs—as if it amplified what her body and soul could give in order to help me get through whatever shit I was dealing with. It wasn't a one-way street either. When she struggled within herself, something inside of me knew. I would hold her, stroke the eye, and feed her soul in a way that I knew only I could.

Closing my eyes, I sank into the moment a little deeper, just for a couple of minutes. This was my favorite part. Not the sex, mind-numbingly fabulous as it was, but this right here. I could feel her shift and start to pull away, though. I don't think she did it consciously; it was a reflex. She'd been so used to shielding herself for so many years. I got that.

"I have to —"

"Shhh." I held her a little bit closer. "I know you have to meet with Gabriel and get your orders, but just give me two more minutes, okay?" I spoke the words against her nape, my mouth never losing contact with her skin. Her hands wrapped around mine, and she pulled them tighter against her body.

"Three," she whispered, squeezing her fingers around mine. I smiled against her skin, and the tattoo hummed in what I could only imagine was approval.

CHAPTER 3
EVELYN

It was never a good sign when the Big G made a personal appearance. He usually phoned orders in to Alex, or whatever it was that he did. Heck, being an archangel and all, he could very well just will the info into someone's head, couldn't he? Regardless of how things normally worked, we weren't exactly in the business of anything close to normal. If Gabriel wanted to meet in person, what was I going to say, no? Right. I could see that conversation going over like a fart in church.

Sitting in silence with Alex in his office, I stared at the blotter as the words he'd spoken to me at the end of the meeting rang like a bell in my head.

"Gabriel is coming...He wants to speak with you himself, Evelyn."

Not that I was afraid of or even intimidated by him or anything. Okay, that was a lie; of course I was intimidated. Who wouldn't be? He was *the* freaking Gabriel, the voice of God and all that shit, for Christ's sake! Every time I was around him, I was that nineteenth-century girl who'd met him on the train all over again. Right out of the nuthouse and scared as all hell, terrified of the situation I'd found myself in and the very real possibility that maybe, just maybe I *was* completely bonkers and everything I'd ever seen and experienced was nothing more than a figment of my imagination. But afraid of him, no. Never of him.

"You are looking quite well, Evelyn. Love suits you."

Crap on a cracker! The sound of Gabriel's voice behind me nearly made me come out of my skin.

"Jeez, we need to put a bell on you or something because you're going to give me a heart attack one of these days with that whole materializing-out-of-nowhere thing you do. Doors, man. Think about it next time."

"Don't be silly. You can't have a heart attack." Gabriel stepped into my peripheral vision a second before he moved over to sit on the corner of Alex's desk in front of me. "And a door?" He chuckled lightly and shook his head. "Where would the fun be in that? You of all people should appreciate that."

He had a point. If I could, I'd pop up behind people just for shits and grins.

"Shall we get to business, then?" He clasped his hands in his lap.

I took a deep breath, then blew it out again, tugging on the end of my braid for good measure. "Ready as I'll ever be."

"I've just been in a meeting, called by Lucifer. Many years ago, he found the Spectoral being, Anabael, in one of the outer Hells—the Simzahnomon Province, to be precise. She worked her way up through his ranks and quickly became one of his favored Spectorals. He trusted her with many of his special possessions, even the Roman emperor Nero, whom she inhabited as the driving force behind his matricide and the brutal murder of his pregnant wife. She was a master at twisting the truth and manipulating people. However, according to Lucifer, she became increasingly insubordinate over time, challenging him at every turn and taking to unsanctioned possessions for her own gain. He states that his concerns regarding Anabael and her growing influence on humankind mirror our own, and he is asking for our help. He also asks that we return her to him directly so he can deal with her as he sees fit."

"And you trust him?" Alex asked. "I mean no disrespect, but you intend to endanger members of my house in a manner that is above and beyond what would normally be asked of them based on what Lucifer says."

Gabriel stood and turned to him, easing his hands into the pockets of his fancy slacks.

"Lucifer may be many things, Alexander, but even he understands that there must be balance. He was my brother once, remember?

"Does he prefer the upper hand? Of course. We all do. However, he knows that if the balance of humanity shifts too far one way or the other, the true meaning of chaos would ensue. And as much as he would thoroughly enjoy the anarchy and insanity that it would bring, he is all too aware that it wouldn't last forever. The destruction of man would be irrevocable, and he would be left with nothing. No followers, no mindless humans, no one at all to create sparks of mischief in his name. Thus, we created a treaty of sorts, guidelines and rules to keep an even and stable human plane because that, above all else, is essential.

"If Anabael is allowed to continue, if her numbers grow any larger than they already are, the world as we know it will come crashing to a cruel and bitter end, and I cannot let that happen. Even if it means handing her over to him when all is said and done. Her death will be brutal, make no mistake. However sensible Lucifer may be, he is still the epitome of malice. I don't enjoy being responsible for the demise of any creature, but this, unfortunately, is unavoidable. According to our treaty, she is his to punish and I…I must bear the knowledge that she was given to him by my hand, and that is *my* burden."

"Of course, my apologies," Alex said with a bow of his head.

"No apology needed." Gabriel looked at me and smiled before turning back to Alex. "You have every right to protect your children. If you didn't question my orders occasionally I would be concerned."

He walked back to the front of the desk and perched on the corner in front of me again.

"As for you, I should tell you that after reviewing all of the hunters in the company and consulting more than a few with the gift of sight, we felt that you were the only clear choice for this assignment. You have the strongest bond with the other hunters of your house, which is going to be imperative for a successful mission. The trust between you all is incomparable. I have watched many a team split apart and move on to different houses as its members 'outgrew' each other. But you evoke something in the people you touch, the members of this house. It is something that cannot be taught or duplicated."

Pfft. Had he forgotten that Lana had taken up residence in our not-so-humble abode?

"I realize that you aren't the closest with the newest hunter, Lana, but even taking that into consideration, the bond within the house is near ironclad. There is no petty competition for lead hunter; the others accept your position and readily support you, and they find that support returned to them — something that I can assure you is not inside every house in the company.

"I also know you, Evelyn, and I know that you will not be thrilled to learn that you will be working extremely closely with Lana. However, I know you will do so without argument, that you are respectful and take what you do for us very seriously, so you will put any differences aside to ensure a successful mission." One of his perfectly sculpted eyebrows cocked up ever so slightly as one side of his mouth kicked up a fraction of an inch.

Damn it. He did know me. If you went by numbers alone, Lana and I should be an excellent partnership, and the few times we'd worked together had been hugely successful. But for whatever reason, she had a bug up her ass where I was concerned, always had and probably always would. What bothered me more, though, was the fact I was still pissed at her for shoving her big Eastern European tongue down Daniel's throat when we'd all first met. Why on earth was I holding on to something so petty? That's really what it was — stupid junior high you-kissed-him-before-I-did crap. I was a hundred and thirty-five years old, for Christ's sake, definitely too old for this shit. I knew all of this on an intellectual level, but could I put it aside on an emotional one to get through this mission?

I had to, plain and simple. Gabriel and Alex trusted her, and I knew without a shadow of a doubt that I trusted them. So, like the good little soldier that I was, I would have to dig out my big-girl panties and have faith that those two knew what they were doing. Maybe by the end of this assignment, Lana and I would be closer for it.

If I lived through this, that was.

That part niggled at the back of my neck. Along with everything else, I had the very distinct feeling one of the other reasons I'd been chosen was because I had the highest probability of making it out alive. Call it a hunch, but I couldn't shake the sensation.

"This mission doesn't have the best odds, does it?" I just had to know.

"Not particularly, no," Gabriel answered.

"Excellent, just how I like it."

"Naturally. You know, the others thought I was insane for recruiting you to begin with." Gabriel grinned at me. Full-on grinned. "Now look at you, one of the most respected hunters—if not *the* most—in the company."

"To say I feel honored feels so inadequate, but it is how I truly feel. I will do everything in my power to make this assignment a success." I bowed my head.

"I know. Your sessions with Lana will begin tomorrow."

"Tomorrow?" I stood and straightened to my fullest height, all five-foot-three inches of me. "I'm ready now."

"I know you are. However, Lana is not. You will need a spiritual partner for this mission, if you will. Due to her psychic abilities and the fact that the two of you have worked well together on other assignments in the past, she is the only one qualified to be that guide for you. There are extensive instructions that I must give her in order for her to do her part and aid you successfully," he explained. "However, you will not be left to your own devices until then. You have an appointment with Tessa. She has a new marking for you."

I looked down at my arms, swathed in ink from wrist to shoulder. My torso, back, and legs were also covered. Every hunter was marked extensively like this. These might look like your average, everyday tattoos slapped on by the local tattoo parlor, at least at first glance, but they were far from anything ordinary. Every drop of ink in our skin was infused with different elements of magic.

Each mark carried with it a spell that assisted hunters with the tools we needed on the fly. Strength, speed, a burst of magic to give us that extra kick we might need to get the job done or to create a distraction so we could get the hell out of a tight spot. The coolest part was that when you called upon the tattoo and that magic started to flow through your veins, the entire piece would glow with power.

I was the house inscriber, and it was nothing short of an honor. Every time someone needed something new, they sat in my chair and I was able to not only create a piece that served the purpose it was meant for but also make it into something more, like a koi fish, night-blooming lily, or a roaring lion. I could take the magic and bend it to my will. Isolde had taught me and my handler Tess that. She'd shown us how to make a spell twist around itself, move in and around the words to become such glorious works of glowing art that any hunter would be proud to carry them on their flesh.

Granted, not every one of my marks could be seen. Some were etched in a pale pink to mimic my natural flesh tone, but that didn't mean I was any less proud of them. I came from a time when women weren't tattooed for beauty, so in order to blend in out in the open, my markings had to be hidden in plain sight. But man, when they lit up, there wasn't an inch of my body that wasn't covered with light.

"Well, I don't know where it'll fit, but I'm sure she'll find someplace," I said and headed out to the shop.

Sitting back in the big black chair in my little tattoo room, I watched Tess get her supplies ready.

"Ya know, it's been, what, fifty years since you've done this. Are you sure you remember how?" I asked.

"Ha-ha, smartass. It's just like riding a bike," she said while whizzing through the prep work as if she'd done it yesterday. "Lose the shirt, sunshine."

"Lose the shirt? Where the hell do you think you're going to put this thing?"

"Honestly, Ev, you really think I don't know where your bare spots are? I could draw a map of your tats, blindfolded, with my feet. Did you forget who slapped about eighty percent of those marks on you? Yours truly. And I'm probably the only person in existence who knows how much you love your tattoos but hate getting them done. Now quit being such a girl, ya wuss, and ditch the bra, too."

With a growl, I ripped my shirt over my head, flung my brassier across the room, and plopped down in the chair. Tess cranked me back, grabbed my left boob, and maneuvered it out of the way to prepare the skin underneath. Great. Tattooed and groped by my best friend in one session. Awesome.

A sigh from the doorway caught my attention, and I popped my head up to see Daniel standing there, grinning like a little boy who just found his dad's *Playboy* stash. He sauntered in, plucked a folded hand towel off the counter, and laid it over my exposed breast.

"In case someone else walks in." He winked and then planted a kiss on my forehead.

"Like there's a person in this house that hasn't seen Ev's boobs."

Daniel laughed and pulled up a stool, taking my hand in his and rubbing his thumb over the back of it. "So how many tattoos do you have, Tess?"

"Um, none, thank you very much. Y'all wanna doodle on yourselves, have at it. Not this chick. That handler brand was enough self-inflicted pain for this gal."

"Now who's the wuss?" I muttered as the buzz of the machine started and the first bite of the needle hit me.

"Damn straight. I'm not even going to pretend otherwise. I have an extremely low tolerance for pain and I own it."

"Ow! Jesus, T, that was bone!"

"Oh, don't be such a baby. Demons try to take your head off on the regular. This should be cake. Suck it up."

There was something different about this tattoo. Perhaps it was the fact that I hadn't been marked in over twenty years, but it hurt like a motherfucker. After an hour of searing pain along my sixth rib, Tess was finally finished. She wiped me down and set ointment on the tray next to Daniel.

"I'll let you handle this part, slugger," she said with a wink, then closed the door of the little room as she left.

CHAPTER 4
DANIEL

As soon as Tess left the room, I picked up the jar of ointment and took a good sized dollop with my fingers. I warmed it in my hands for a moment before applying it to Evie's silky skin with the gentlest of touches. I tried to keep my face calm—I mean, rubbing up on my girlfriend's half-naked body wasn't exactly an arduous task, but there *was* something bothering me, something I couldn't quite put into words just yet, mostly because I didn't want to sound like a huge pussy. I'd all but decided to keep my mouth shut when my eyes met hers, and suddenly it felt like I didn't have to tell her; she already knew. The words came out anyway.

"I have a bad feeling about this mission," I said quietly. "I can't explain how or why it feels any worse than any other assignment, but it just does. I wasn't freaked out this much when we went in after Mzetir, and even you have to admit that was seriously hairy. And before you say anything, it has nothing to do with you going into this assignment alone either. We've been there and done that before, and while it sucked ass, I didn't feel like this. Even after I saw what that rat bastard Chilgaz did to you, it wasn't this bad. There's something in my gut that I can't shake, Ev, no matter how hard I try to rationalize or ignore it, and it scares the shit out of me."

Whew. There, I'd said it. All my pussy chips were out on the table.

"I know," she whispered, pulling my face down to hers.

She kissed me, ferocious and hard. The passion behind this kiss didn't have the usual sexual undertones that laced an after-assignment lip-lock, however. I answered back, wordlessly pleading with the same desperate intensity she was giving me. It wasn't going to be enough, I knew that—she probably did too—but it had to help. Something had to help unravel the feelings of despair knotting my gut.

The next morning, I slipped out of bed before Evie woke up and headed down to the basement. I needed to talk to Alex. It was so ridiculously early that when I passed through the kitchen it was still dark, which meant that Isolde wasn't even up yet. I continued down the stairs into the basement and wondered if Alex was awake or if I'd find an empty office.

As I passed the tech lab, I saw Tony hunched over a table, looking through one of those big magnifying lamps. This wasn't surprising as he was resident nerd, which was all kinds of an oxymoron. The dude looked like one of those professional cage fighters and at first glance appeared to have taken one too many blows to the head. But, as they say, looks can be deceiving, and Tony was the epitome of that saying.

"Hey, man, what are you doing up at this ungodly hour?" He wore a pair of glasses that made his eyes look so comically large I couldn't help but laugh every time.

"Just got some shit in my head I need to work out. Thought I'd talk to Alex about it."

"Is there anything I can do?" he asked as he pulled his glasses off and set his equipment on the table. "Look, this job has some massively hard parts to it, and you got dealt a serious blow yesterday."

"There's nothing anyone can do, really. I mean, this is the job, right? I don't know why I'm even bothering to go talk to him. What am I going to do?" I shrugged. "Evie's going out there on some assignment that has *her* scared, and I'm supposed to stay back here at the house, sit on my hands and just let it happen? Could you do it? Could you turn your back on Josie and let her go out there to face this Spectoral thing?"

By the time I'd finished, I was panting and waving my hands around the tech lab like a lunatic.

"First off, you're not turning your back on Evie, so tell *that* train of thought to leave the station. Second, sit on your hands? Man, seriously? Do you really think Alex is going to make you sit in the corner and just watch as this whole thing, whatever it is, goes down? Trust me, you'll probably be working harder than anyone else, other than Evie herself. And third, I feel for you, brother, I really, truly do, and I get that you're freaking out and need to flail. But can you not do it right next to the table of little, tiny computer parts?"

"Sorry." I shoved my hands in my pockets.

"I'm kidding. Hey, if it will help you to knock all this shit to the ground—"

"Nah," I said with a small, half-hearted laugh. "I wish it would, though."

"I can't imagine what you must be going through right now. My brain hurts just trying to wrap around how in the hell *you're* going to wrap your head around this assignment."

"Yeah, I'm hoping that maybe Alex can work some of his reassurance mojo on me so I can get a handle on all of this."

"Good luck, and if there's anything I can do—a punching bag to let off steam or if you just want to talk—I'm here. We all are."

"Thanks, that really does help."

When I turned to leave the tech lab, I peeked down the hallway to make sure Alex was in. The light that shone through the cracked open door answered that question. Not shocking, really; the guy practically slept in that office.

I knocked on the door as I gave it a little shove, only to see Gabriel perched on the corner of Alex's desk.

"Oh shit, sorry, I'll come back." I backed out into the hallway.

"No, Daniel, please. Come in." Gabriel stood, sweeping his arm to the empty chair on the other side of Alex's desk. "We were waiting on you, actually."

"O-kaaay…" I cautiously took the seat offered.

"Relax, you aren't in any kind of trouble," Alex said, and I could feel a bit of the tension in my body release.

"Your concern at the moment isn't about your state, is it?" Gabriel rested a hand on my shoulder; his touch was warm and comforting.

I shook my head. "No."

"You're worried about Evelyn." Alex leaned back in his chair, pressing his palms together.

"I know she's been out on more assignments by herself than I've been on assignments in my life, and I know that she's the most capable hunter in this house, probably in the entire company, but…" The words stuck, and I had to swallow a couple of times to loosen them up. "I love Evelyn, I love her more than I ever thought I could love anything, and I can't…" My throat closed around the words I was about to say; I was terrified that if I spoke them out loud, they would somehow come to fruition. I took a deep breath and tried to shake the words free. "I can't lose her. I understand that it's a possibility. It's always a possibility. I get that, and I'm always aware of it whenever the two of us are apart for assignments. But this mission is different. I can't explain how I know that it is. I just do."

Gabriel smiled. It was strange and kind of maddening to see that reaction to me pouring my heart out. He must have sensed my aggravation, because he shook his head.

"Please, do not take my response as a slight to how you are feeling. It is anything but," he said. "It is only that I am reminded of another hunter who would and *has* behaved in a manner very similar to yours at the moment."

He glanced at Alex, who straightened in his chair and adjusted his tie.

"That is neither here nor there," Alex said, clearing his throat.

"On the contrary, I believe it to be here *and* there, and I believe our young friend could very well benefit from your experience, Alexander."

"Very well," Alex said, albeit reluctantly. "As you well know, I was a hunter many years ago, but what you do not know was that I worked with the most glorious creature, a woman so fierce and intelligent that all of my skills paled next to the things she could do. She could smite a foe with such grace and artistry that I marveled at her abilities every time we went out." He stood from his seat and crossed to the small window just past his office door. The blinds were closed, but he stared pensively at them as if he could see right through them.

"From the moment I saw her, standing on the beach on the Isle of Anglesey on the northwest coast of Wales, I knew. After she'd finished relieving a Nicoron demon of his head, she stomped across the sand to me and demanded to know where I'd been. Turned out she'd seen me in a vision and had been on that beach for three days waiting for me." He smiled to himself and shook his head. "My apologies. That wasn't really relevant to your situation, was it? Nevertheless, every moment I was in her presence, the more hopelessly in love with her I fell. There wasn't a thing I wouldn't do to stay with her and keep her safe, even though I knew she was more than capable of the latter.

"Gabriel came to us one spring morning and informed us that he needed her assistance as a theurgist to perform a spell for a group of hunters going after a deadly Spectoral—Anabael, in fact. The horror that filled my body the closer we drew to the end of our journey is something that no other person could understand, a sense of dread so dire and whole that I was physically sick with it. I pled with Gabriel for a reprieve, to find another hunter to perform the spell needed, but there was no other. I had to watch as the woman I loved walked into the lion's den, never knowing if she would come out alive or if she would be eaten."

Alex turned away from the window, hands clasped behind his back. I could almost see the memory ripple through him.

"What happened?" I asked after he'd been quiet for a few moments.

"Well—" he caught his breath, as if snapping back to the present "—as we are currently in pursuit of Anabael, I'd say the mission was decidedly unsuccessful."

"Jesus, Alex, I don't know what to say other than this isn't making me feel any better about all of this."

"No, you misunderstand." He shook his head and waved off my condolences. "We did lose that day, lost six very great hunters indeed, but the woman I speak of is very much alive. As a matter of fact, she should be upstairs preparing today's breakfast at any moment."

Isolde? Shit. I flopped back in the chair, my hand pressed to my forehead to keep my head from spinning right off.

Gabriel drew my attention when he sat on the edge of Alex's desk in front of me. "I wanted Alexander to share that with you because he is the reason Isolde did not perish with the other hunters that day. His bond with her, a bond very much like the one you share with Evelyn, is the only reason she is still alive. You see, what Alexander has with Isolde, what you have with Evelyn, is something that is more powerful than any angelical gift I can bestow upon you."

CHAPTER 5
EVELYN

The next morning when I woke up, I noticed that Daniel had already gone. He was probably in the training room, so I was going to try to get in a quick workout with him before meeting with Lana.

When I opened my bedroom door at the same time she opened hers, I knew that wasn't going to happen. We stared at each other in the middle of the hallway.

"I was coming to look for you," she said. "We have a lot of work to do and should be getting started."

I nodded. "You're right. Let's do this thing."

We walked down the stairs and into the basement in silence. We hadn't done more than glance in each other's direction, and the air between us seemed to be pulled tight with tension. When we got to her office, the room next to my shop, I had to admit I was taken aback. I didn't really know what I'd expected to see—a dartboard with my picture in the middle of it, perhaps—but I wasn't prepared for this.

The light inside was soft and almost dreamy. The smell of burning incense washed over me, but it was soothing, not overpowering, and kind of made me feel relaxed and sated in a strange way. A few canvas hammock-style sling chairs were in the middle of the room, and a giant beanbag big enough for three sat in one corner. I turned around to see the other side of the space and had to hold back a gasp.

Drawings covered the wall — black swirls and smudges of charcoal, all of them erratic and unkempt except for one element, one spot on the paper that made sense yet didn't at the same time. An eyeball, a finger, a portion of a mouth. Even a table, set so low to the ground that you would have to sit or squat down to use it, was littered with drawings, bits of broken charcoal, and dust.

"These are much better than before," Lana said, walking up next to me. "Before I came here, before Isolde helped me, I couldn't grasp anything, only blackness. My other visions were clear, and I could draw them as if I created them. But these…I would try to capture something, force myself to scribble until my fingers bled and I lost consciousness, only to wake up and find page after page of nothing."

"Jesus, Lana, I had no idea."

"If it was not for this mission, you never would have," she said quietly. "Only Maria, and then Isolde, knew of my torment." She turned to me. "I know that we have had many differences in our past. I admit to feeling great jealousy when it comes to you. You excel in everything you do, and there is no effort to it. You simply do it. Part of me hates you for that, but a larger part envies your abilities, the devotion and support you have from everyone inside this house — from Daniel, Gabriel, even myself." She took a moment to compose herself before she continued.

"There are a few things about this assignment that I am certain of, and one that has been clear in my mind, that has shone through all of the darkness and shadow, is that you are the only one who can stop Anabael. I have also seen what happens if she continues on her path, the desolate world that is left over after she has consumed all things, the nightmare of what is left in her wake. All of humanity will be obliterated, do you understand? If she succeeds, there will be nothing left, Evelyn, nothing at all. No good, no bad…nothing. One more thing that has remained clear to me is that I am the only one who can truly help you do it. In order for that to happen, you must have trust in me, and for you to have trust in me, you must know all parts of me." Lana gestured to her wall. "Even the parts I don't want anyone to see."

Suddenly I felt like a complete ass.

"Lana…"

"No, please, I know you have been upset with me because of my initial actions with Daniel. I apologize for that. My only explanation is that I had seen the vision of you two together before I came to the house. It wasn't as if I wanted him, you must believe me, but you had so much already, I — I didn't want you to have him, too."

Everything clicked into place inside my head, and I couldn't help but laugh. I really tried to hold it in, but it was like trying to stop a sneeze.

"This is amusing to you?" She sounded hurt and pissed. I could literally feel the anger and tension radiating off of her.

"No," I choked out. "God no, it's that it just hit me." She didn't seem to understand, and I had to catch my breath in order to explain. "Don't you get it, the ridiculousness of it all? You and me, jealous of each other, over things that are absolutely out of our control."

"You envy me?" she asked with a look that I could only describe as completely gobsmacked. "What could I possibly possess that *you* would covet?"

I cocked an eyebrow at her. "You own a mirror, right?" I gestured to her entire body. "I mean, look at you: tall, blond, and gorgeous with that whole Boris-and-Natasha accent thing going on. You look and sound like you just stepped out of some guy's wet dream and into reality, for shit's sake."

"You are jealous over my beauty? That is —"

"Petty and positively redonkulous? Yeah, I know, but believe it or not, that's not the worst of it." Her eyes got as big as saucers, and my stomach clenched. Jesus, this was going to be a helluva lot harder to admit out loud to myself, let alone to her. But if she could let it all hang out, then so could I, and there was only one way to do this. Like a ripping off a bandage — quick. "I was jealous because you kissed Daniel before I did."

There, it was all out in the open, exposed to the air. The room was silent, and Lana and I stared at each other for a good several seconds before we both started to laugh. It was as if the weight and animosity between us lifted a little more with every knee slap and belly grab. I could feel myself opening up, letting Lana peek behind the wall that I had worked so hard to keep up around me. And damn it, I liked the warm sensation of letting someone new in.

"I don't know how you do it, girl." I gestured to all of the drawings. "Hunting with all that shit running around in your head. That's nuts."

The smile on her face melted into one of the grimmest looks I'd ever seen in my life. She took a deep breath and let it out slowly.

"I have not hunted in over ten years."

Those eight little words were like a giant vacuum, sucking the light humor out of the room and replacing it with humiliation, disappointment, and hurt. I reacted on instinct, pulling her into an embrace and holding her tight. Her shoulders shook with sobs as her body sagged against mine, and she clenched her hands, crumpling the back of my shirt in her fists. My gut wrenched and tears stung the back of my own eyes, spilling over and running down my cheeks as I imagined what life would be like without hunting, without purpose. It would be worse than anything I could fathom, and worse than death itself.

A strange sensation tingled along my rib, across the new tattoo. Something must have triggered its glow, but it didn't feel like any of my other hunter marks; it felt more like the Eye on the back of my neck, warm and almost buzzing. Lana must have felt it as well because she took a step back. Oddly enough, she smiled through her tears, wiping them away in wonder as she looked at the glow radiating out from under my shirt. There was an audible hum in the room, and it took me a second to realize that the sound wasn't just coming from me. A light began to shine through the fabric of Lana's sheer blouse, a thin line under her left breast that mimicked the shape and location of my newest tattoo.

"What is this?" I asked, fingering my own vibrating skin.

"It's an old charm," Isolde's voice floated into the room. "Many years ago, it was placed upon every member in a house to bond them. However, as we evolved as hunters and began to interchange among the houses, it became obsolete." As she spoke, I noticed a glow emanating from her as well—she clearly carried the mark. There was only one way for this to be possible.

"Isolde, I've known you for more than a hundred years. I never knew…" The words stuck in the back of my throat somehow.

"That I am a hunter? No, you couldn't have. By the time Alexander and I took you in, I had been out of the field for several centuries. The visions I had were much like Lana's—all-consuming, rendering it dangerous to continue hunting as I had before. So, as with most hunters that have the sight, I had to retire from outside assignments. It was hard in the beginning, but we learn to adjust and use our other skills to become hunters in a different way. You see, we hunt in the spiritual and psychological realm whereas you continue to do your work in the physical one. It is a different mindset that Lana is still adapting to, and naturally she mourns the loss of her previous way of life. But this isn't about her or me. We are here for you. I don't think you realize what you are sacrificing on this mission."

"Come on, Iz, you know better than anyone that as a hunter I put my life on the line every time I walk out the door. This isn't anything different."

"Oh, but it is. You see, if you fail, it won't be your life that you lose."

"I don't understand."

"As you know, Anabael is a Spectoral, and if this mission isn't successful, if she gets inside of you, you could very well lose your mind. Believe me, that is far worse than losing your life, for you won't know what you do." She took a breath and swallowed hard, as if she were remembering something horrible or just trying not to hork up bad sushi. "I have seen it. I have seen what happens if everything goes pear-shaped. You won't just destroy yourself, you will be the destruction of everyone and everything. Evelyn, you will be the end of humanity as we know it."

Before that nugget of information could sink in, a loud shriek from my tattoo room next door penetrated the wall. I knew that screech, too — only one person on the planet made that ungodly sound…Tessa. My handler was in trouble, and my brain sent my body into action.

Practically shoving Isolde out of the way, I bolted, gripping the doorframe and catapulting myself into the hallway as I rounded the corner. I scrambled to make a hard right into my shop, and everyone in the house was crowded around its open door, standing on tiptoe and craning their necks to see inside.

"Move!" I shouted, punching my way past Tony and Z, hip checking Josie and Daniel, and practically body slamming Daniel's handler Chris into the wall with only one thought on my mind: *Get to Tess.*

"Stop!" Alex said in his serious boss-man voice, and I skidded to a halt, managing to stop myself just short of attacking him.

Jesus. In my knee-jerk reaction to defend my handler, even if it was from Alex, I almost hadn't seen the tattoo gun in his hand or realized he was marking Tess. He wiped over her sixth rib on the left, and as the cloth moved, it revealed the glowing charm that was on me, Lana, and Isolde.

The hum I'd heard in the other room started again, growing louder and louder as it rolled through the air and made the little potion vials in the next room rattle with its intensity and power. As I looked up, everyone began to raise their shirts, one by one uncovering a brightly lit, extremely fresh bonding charm. Even the other handlers that I hadn't noticed behind Tony and Z had them.

Words escaped me completely, probably for the first time in my life. I knew we were all tight, but this was going above and beyond to the nth degree. Turning to Alex again, I noticed the same light shone under his left pec, barely visible behind his layers of shirt. He set the tattoo gun down on the tray, next to the inkwell Tess had used on me; it was one I hadn't seen before that day, and now I could see that it was a very old glass pot, not one of the disposable ones I used.

"Close your mouth, genius. You're gonna catch flies," Tessa said as she rolled her shirt down over her charm.

Isolde's arm came around my shoulders, and I immediately flinched at the contact before letting her familiar calm sink into me as she spoke.

"Initially, we marked Lana because it was necessary for this assignment to be successful and Daniel because we needed someone who was bonded to your heart and soul. However, when the others learned of what was at stake, what you are risking, they all *insisted* on being marked with the bonding charm as well. The ink is the same that was used on Alexander and myself over a thousand years ago; it works with the tattoo to create an impossibly strong connection. We are all linked to one another, in this plane of existence and the next."

"Lana and Daniel, I understand," I said quietly. "Hell, I even understand you and Alex, but everyone else—?" My mind reeled, trying to grasp the whole of what had been done, the weight of it.

"Your humility and inability to understand why they would all do this for you is precisely *why* they did this," Isolde said. "They have marked themselves in an effort to help protect you."

My throat squeezed in on itself as I fought to hold back immense emotion. Straightening my back and taking a deep breath, I managed to eke out a semi-normal-sounding "Thank you."

CHAPTER 6
DANIEL

It amazed me that she didn't get it. After all the years Evie had worked with the people in the house, she still didn't understand the love they had for her. It wasn't just the other hunters that respected her either; their handlers held her in high regard as well.

"All right everyone, get the hell out of here before she blows and we're all in the splash zone," Tess announced, shooing everyone from the room except me. "You can stay," she said as she shot me wink and shut the door behind her. She was truly Evie's best friend and knew as well as I did that the last thing Evs wanted to do was break down in front of everyone.

As the latch clicked closed, I looked over to see Evie trembling.

"You okay?" I asked, knowing damn well she was going to lie and tell me she was fine.

She only nodded, her teeth clenching so tight the muscles in her jaw bulged.

"You sure?"

I didn't know why I'd bothered to ask that. Even after all we'd been through together, she still wouldn't admit to any weaknesses. So I did the only thing that might make her crack a little bit — I crossed the room and wrapped my arms around her. She was stiff as a board against me, utterly unyielding other than the trembling.

"You really didn't know how much they all love and respect you, did you?"

All she did was shake her head against my shoulder in response.

"Do you now?"

I felt her hands creep up my back and grip my shoulders as she nodded emphatically. Tears soaked my shirt as the dam of her emotions overflowed. She kept so much pent up against the world, and I didn't know why.

Okay, that wasn't true. I knew why. Her mind was in a constant state of survival mode, an endless barrage of wall building to keep everyone out in order to protect herself. It made loving her harder, and I was sure it had turned her little world on its ear when I'd first shown up that day in Alex's office like a sledgehammer that broke down her defenses. Honestly, I thought that was why she'd hated me so much in the beginning. I would never forget — the moment she'd stepped in the room, sparks had ignited between us, and that had pissed her off something fierce.

Working slowly to not break the moment, I managed to get us over to the chair in the middle of the room and pulled her into my lap. I cradled her there, holding her close and feeling her body melt as she gave in to the comfort and safety I offered.

"Don't tell anyone about this, okay?" she said into my neck.

"And ruin your street cred with the other hunters? You know I wouldn't do that. Besides, I know you'd kick my ass if I did."

She laughed softly and snuggled against me a little deeper. I loved her this way. Soft, vulnerable, and open.

Don't get me wrong, her hunter side was a force to be reckoned with. She wasn't a shrinking violet who cowered in the corner, waiting for someone to come and save her. Not even a little bit. She did the saving. When she was out there fighting a demon, Divinity blade in hand and tattoos glowing all over her body, she looked like what I imagined Athena, the Greek goddess of war, looked like. Strong, sure, and deadly: the trifecta of hotness that was the envy of so many men.

But *I* got to take her home. I got to lay her down on our bed and make love to her. I was the only one whom she allowed to strip her layers of armor away to see the woman underneath the hunter. The scared, unsure woman who cared so deeply for those around her that she held herself at arm's length in hope that no one would get close enough, because she knew the dangers of this job. However, in her insistence that she didn't need comforting, she was blind to the times she comforted others.

When a human was killed on an assignment we'd shared, I was devastated even though he'd been working with the demons. But Evie had been there, talking me out of my own head, assuring me that I hadn't put the man in the line of danger; he'd put himself there. She'd lain next to me and let me hold her all night just so I could feel normal for a little while. I had felt normal, too, because she'd opened up—just a crack, but enough to let me peek in. I'd known then and there, lying on that little twin bed in that dark room with her spooned up against me, that I'd never love another the way I loved her.

"I know we have a meeting with Alex, but do you think he'd mind if we hung out here a little bit longer?" She wrapped her arms around me a little bit tighter. "I—I'm—" Her tears started up again, and she shook her head in what I knew was frustration. "Damn it, why can't I stop this?"

"Shhh, babe, it's okay. Take all the time you need."

Evie craned her head back to look up at me. "Will you stay with me?"

"Always."

She looked like a hot mess. Her nose was red and running, her eyes bloodshot, and there were stands of hair plastered to her face with tears. I reached across and yanked a tissue out of the box on the little tray table. I dabbed at the wetness on her face and held it up for her as she blew her nose.

Definitely always.

CHAPTER 7
EVELYN

It took a while to compose myself. I'd never been so touched, on such a level, in my entire life, and it was a feeling that filled every corner of me, from the top of my head to the tips of my toes. How does one compensate for that kind of dedication?

Not dying would be a good start, I supposed.

When my emotions finally stabilized, Alex called me and Daniel into his office. As we stepped into the large room, I saw Gabriel standing behind the mahogany desk with guess who parked in the corner, leaning against the wall...Lucifer. Mister Big, evil and pretty.

"Holy shit," Daniel said, freezing where he stood in the doorway.

"Well, I've been called much worse." A sly, unholy smile spread across Lucifer's face, twisting the corners of his mouth up unnaturally. His hair was cut much shorter than the last time I'd seen the bastard but still just as jet black as sin itself and combed back off his forehead. The piercing, bright green of his eyes darted from Daniel to me, and his smile melted away. I swear his upper lip came to perfect points under his turned-up nose. My heart skipped a beat at the sight of him. Not from adoration but fear — pure, unadulterated fear.

And that freaking asshole knew it.

I could almost feel him picking through my brain, looking for something to poke at. His nostrils flared and his full bottom lip thinned, spreading when the grin returned as if he'd pinpointed an insecurity to exploit. The alabaster skin around his eyes seemed to pull back into his skull as the stare pinned me to the carpet. He took a step in my direction, and my instincts screamed at me to run, but I rooted myself to the floor and refused to move; it was bad enough he knew I was scared. He moved right up in my space and leaned in.

"Always a pleasure, Evelyn," he purred into my ear. He drew out the syllables of my name like he reveled in the sound they made coming out of his mouth, and he was so close that I could feel the cold brush of his lips on my skin.

Light erupted in the room, and I heard a growling sound to my right: Daniel.

"Back. The fuck. Off," Daniel warned, his teeth bared — *bared*, for God's sake. "Satan or not, I will kick your ass if you don't leave her alone this instant."

Arching a perfectly sculpted black eyebrow, Lucifer leaned around me and looked at Daniel. I mean, who in their right mind would challenge the devil like that? Okay, I probably would, but I had a sense of what this joker could do and what I could get away with. Daniel didn't, and I don't think he cared. Loathing radiated from him, and being this close to Luce, I could feel him drinking in Daniel's anger; the bastard fed off of rage and discord of any kind. But knowing the dickhead, the disrespect Daniel showed him was getting old fast. After a few minutes, when Daniel still stood his ground and didn't budge an inch, Lucifer rolled his eyes and sighed.

"Honestly, you people let me have no fun at all. And my name is Lucifer, thank you very much. Satan has no…panache." He slunk back to his corner. "The boy's bond to her is strong, the strongest I've seen in a very long time."

Gabriel nodded. "Indeed." The two of them looked at each other with what could only be unspoken communication.

"What's going on?" I asked. "I've just been bonded to everyone in the house. What does Daniel's bond to me have to do with anything?"

Alex took off his glasses and cleaned them with the little handkerchief he'd pulled out of his pocket. "The connection you have with Daniel, or more specifically, the connection he has to *you*, is different than what you have with anyone else, even your handler Tessa. And it could very well be an extremely vital component in the success of this mission."

"Then I'm in. What do I have to do?" Daniel asked without a second of hesitation.

"Your passion and dedication to Evelyn is truly honorable, Daniel," Gabriel said, "but you must take a moment to consider what we are about to ask you—"

"I don't care what it is, I'll do it. Hell, I'll do it twice, three times if I need to."

The sound of slow clapping filled the room, emanating from Lucifer's corner. "Bravo, young sir." His smile dripped with saccharine, sweet but sickeningly so. "However, this isn't only your decision to make. Your lovely lady fair has a say in it as well." He winked at me, and it truly made my skin crawl.

"Would someone please tell me what's going on? What decision?" I pounded the desk for good measure, which I immediately regretted. I could see Luce's icy green eyeballs widen, sucking in my frustration and lapping it up.

"What Lucifer is alluding to," Gabriel began, "is a pagan ritual that we haven't supported in some time. However, in this case, Alexander and I feel that we would be remiss if we did not allow the two of you to consider...the Soul Binding Circle."

My mouth fell open. Literally. Gape-ass, fly-catching open.

"You can't be serious," I said once I'd finally regained the ability to talk. "I thought you guys didn't do that anymore. Shit, it hasn't been done in over a thousand years."

"One thousand, two hundred and ninety-three years, to be precise." Lucifer crossed his arms over his chest and looked off into the distance. "Ah, yes, I remember it well. Didn't work out too well for your people, did it, Brother? But then again, they didn't have the initial bond that these two have, did they?"

"No," Gabriel said, his voice tight with a hint of something I'd never heard from him before—anger.

My hackles prickled as a memory flooded back to me.

As a new hunter, I had found the ritual in an old book and asked Alex about it. The story he'd told had stuck with me. The tale was about a battle with Anabael—imagine that—before she'd broken away from Lucifer's rule, one that no one would ever find in any text anywhere, not even in the backlogs of Lebriga. I imagined that Alex would never have even told me the story if I hadn't found the ritual by accident.

The fight had been long and horribly brutal, the hunters involved driven so completely insane that Gabriel had no choice but to put them down and out of their misery himself. In an effort to corner Anabael, an unprecedented level of bonding had been done. Six hunters, carefully chosen from around the world as one massive ritual bonded them to each other by blood and soul. Three would go in, the strongest fighters — Fausta, Andreas, and Serverus. They would enter the lair she'd been holed up in and dispatch her when the others of her crew had vacated the bodies they were in. She would be alone and vulnerable. Three would stay behind, the most cunning of wit — Tarquin, Livia, and Verina — and prepare to latch on to the other souls should they fall into possession.

Naturally they had, and Anabael escaped unscathed. The three had come back into Gabriel's fold, each with a mind that wasn't their own, and when the other three had attempted to free their minds, insanity beset them all. It had been like a disease, sweeping over them in a domino effect — one right after the other, mad as a hatter. They'd started in on each other, fighting amongst themselves with words and then fists before turning on themselves, clawing at their own flesh with blunt nails. Half a dozen hunters had been rendered useless in one fell swoop, all because of Anabael and all because they'd been bound at the soul, linked on a level so deep that even Gabriel could not reach them.

My brain started bubbling with doubt. What if this assignment went sour? Would I go mad and drag Daniel down onto the crazy train with me? Did I really want to put him in that kind of danger knowing full well he'd do it just because I asked him to?

Did I really have a choice?

Apprehension must have been written all over my face, because the next thing I knew, Gabriel was standing in front of me, taking my hand in his. "The hunters in the past were too many and not of the same house. It was a mistake that I must bear for the rest of eternity and is the reason why we stopped performing the ritual. You and Daniel are different. There is a connection between you two that is one of the strongest I've ever seen, and if your mind is taken, he has the best chance of getting it back. If I thought for one moment that you and Daniel could not handle this, I wouldn't even propose it to you. Do you understand? I also want you to know that this is only an *option* and we can most certainly do this without the ritual."

"And the odds for success are considerably less, but only for me, right? No harm will come to Daniel if we don't do this?"

"Yes." Gabriel nodded.

Daniel sidled up next to me, and I felt his arm snake around my waist. "Hey, don't worry about me, okay? I may not be as old as you, but I'm big boy and can handle myself. You gotta know that if something happens to you and there was anything I could have done to stop it and didn't…do you really think I could live with myself? I can see that whatever this ritual is has you scared shitless, and that's okay. I got you and I'm in. Nine hundred percent, balls-to-the-wall in, baby, always," he said with that panty-melting grin.

I had to laugh. Had the roles been reversed, I would have said the exact same thing. Clearly there was only one way this would go down.

"All right, then it's settled. Let's do this thing."

"Honestly, I don't know why you don't perform this ritual more often. I'll bring the popcorn," Lucifer said, slapping his hands together and rubbing them vigorously with glee.

"No," Gabriel barked. "This will just be Evelyn, Daniel, Lana, and Isolde. No handlers, no superior beings. This is an intimate and sacred ritual requiring only the participants and the two who shall recite the incantation."

"Damn. I was hoping that since I had behaved today, for the most part, I could be invited into what is certain to be a delicious hunter sandwich." Lucifer closed his eyes and hummed with pleasure.

"Enough!" Alex slammed his fist on his desk so hard his cup full of pens fell over. "I will not take one more moment of your filth in my home."

"Agreed." Gabriel strode over to Lucifer, placed a hand on his chest, and the two of them vanished as if they'd never been there.

Daniel shook his head. "You're right, he *is* a complete douche."

CHAPTER 8
DANIEL

After Lucifer and Gabriel had dematerialized right before our eyes, or whatever the hell it was they'd done to poof into nothingness, Alex sat Evie and I down to explain the particulars of this whole Soul Binding Circle spell thing.

The basics of the ritual were this: Evie and I stood in the center of the soul binding circle and cut each other with our Divinity blades to bond the blood between us while Lana and Isolde walked around the outside of the circle reciting the incantation that made it all work.

"That sounds simple enough," I said. I mean, I didn't like the idea of having to injure Evs in any way, but if it would help save her ass, I was down.

"Yes, that is the simple part." Alex started to pace behind his desk. He looked — I don't know — nervous, for lack of a better word. But that couldn't be; Alex was the coolest cat in the world. I don't even think the word *nervous* was in his vocabulary. "In addition to the blood bond, there must be an act of —" he took out a handkerchief and wiped his brow "— coupling."

"Coupling? Again, I don't see what's so hard about this. We're a couple."

"He means sex," Evie whispered to me. "You and I have to have —"

"Sex? What, right there in front of Lana and Isolde?" Alex and Evie both nodded. "Wow, way to put pressure on a guy to perform."

"Daniel, if you are uncertain in any way, you must say your peace now and we will figure out another way to protect Evelyn," Alex said. "You both must complete the spell *willingly* or it will not work."

"Like hell. I'm not backing out, don't worry about me. I'm still in this."

The next morning I found myself standing in the middle of Lana's office space with Evelyn, the calming scent of white lotus incense wafting all around us. I clutched my Divinity blade and held the sash that kept my robe closed while I stared at the circle of candles.

We were really doing this, weren't we?

I mean, the logistics of the ritual seemed simple enough. We activated our blades, drew blood, bonded through the blood, and in the middle of all of that had some sexy times. It's not like it wasn't something we didn't do, a lot. It was the in-front-of-an-audience part that made me feel sketchy.

Granted, it was only an audience of two. I could do this; I was up for it. I just hoped like hell Little Dan was on board, too. If he didn't cooperate, this ritual wasn't going very far.

Isolde stopped us before we began. "Before you enter the circle, I want to make sure that you are both clear on what's going to happen and that you're okay with it, because once you enter there's no coming out until it's done."

I looked at the candles and ceremonial rug laid out on the floor.

"If I understand it right," I said, "she has to enter with me willingly or it isn't going to work."

"Correct."

"Daniel, you don't have to —"

"The hell I don't. If I can't be out there with you, then I'm sure as shit going to do anything and everything I can to make sure you come back to me. If your mind is taken, if you come back not...you, I'll be the first one to know it. And you know damn well I'm the only one who can crack through that thick-ass head of yours. Believe me, if you're in there at all, I'll find you. Besides, if for whatever reason I can't get you back out, I'd go batshit crazy without you, so we might as well make it official."

"I—"

"Don't rationalize it, don't get wrapped up inside your own head. All I need is a yes or no. Heck, I'll settle for a nod." God, my voice sounded so desperate, but shit, I *was* desperate.

She took a deep breath and nodded once.

And we're off.

Without hesitation, before I could even let myself have any glimmer of a second thought, I threw off my robe and held my hand out to her. Watching her shrug out of her own covering, I felt more naked than I'd ever felt in my entire life, but I was oddly okay with it. I *could* do this—*we* could do this. She took my offered hand, and I led her into the center of the circle. As Lana and Isolde started to move around us, quietly muttering the spell, I felt her body tense.

"Don't worry about them. Just look at me, okay?" I stood directly in front of her in an attempt to block everything from her vision but me. I needed to be her strength, her ability to go through this, her reason for coming back from any mission, this one included. I didn't know how I knew all of this, but I did, and I needed to make sure she could feel it, too. "We can do this."

Holding up my Divinity blade, I sliced one palm and then the other—one to activate my blade and the other for her.

She followed my lead and did the same, her eyes completely focused on mine. I could see the trepidation in them and had to alleviate that.

"Close your eyes," I whispered. "We can do this. If there are any two people in this house who can, it's us. Listen to the sound of my voice. Concentrate on the way I sound, on the way my voice makes you feel." I moved around her as I spoke, surrounding her with my presence. I let her feel the warmth of my breath behind her to let her know where I was, and as my lips moved against the shell of her ear, I began to paint a picture for her with my words. "Imagine that we are the only two creatures in this room, in the whole world." I let my hands move up her sides, and the sensation surprised her. I liked touching her with one hand still wrapped around my blade; the energy from it sparked between our skin as I bent and kissed the Eye on the back of her neck.

She gasped at the contact, arching back toward me, and I could feel my own body responding, hardening as hers began to hum for me, literally. The awareness was all-consuming, powerful. When we were together like this, I was sure of everything I did. She was truly mine, mind, body, and soul.

"Yes," I sighed. I could practically hear her thoughts, the desire building between us. I planted slow, open-mouthed kisses on her shoulder, dragging the tips of my fingers down her bare, taut belly.

My tattoos blasted to life, tingling under my skin, and I could hear the candles around us crackle and whoosh as their heat licked at my naked body.

"Will you honor me?" I asked in another language. How did I know these words?

Her body slid against mine, urging my hand lower. I gripped her tight between her legs, feeling those deliciously damp folds welcome me, and I forgot to care how I knew that language and why. I worked my fingers inside of her relentlessly, forcing her body to go utterly limp. She leaned against me for support, arms splayed out, thighs shaking as my arousal pressed hot and hard against her back. I could hear Isolde and Lana chanting around us, the same phrase over and over again; the cadence of it was almost hypnotic and made me feel woozy. I needed Evelyn, now.

"May I complete this ritual and bind my soul to yours before these witnesses?"

"Yes," she choked out, between gulps of air.

In a matter of seconds I had released my hold, spun her in my arms, and pulled her to the floor, into my lap. With a desperation that made my hands shake, I wrapped her legs around my waist and held myself up as she glided down over my erection. We both stopped breathing for a second as I was finally buried deep inside of her. Jesus Christ, this was, and always would be, my heaven.

As if my arms had a mind of their own, I instinctively raised my sword over her back and made a quick slice, feeling the burn on my own back as she did the same. Pressing the open wound on my palm to the fresh blood between her shoulder blades, my body jolted with sensation.

"Oh God," she breathed as we started to rock, my palm pushing against her back as if I was trying to work my way under her skin. Slowly and rhythmically, our tattoos pulsed in tandem with our hearts; even the candles around us flickered in unison. Warmth began to spread from my spine, and I could feel her blood moving with mine, making its way through my veins, flowing through my arteries, into my heart, and down into my soul. She was everywhere. I was inside of her and she was, in a sense, inside of me. I could taste her in my mouth and smell her scent from within myself. It was strange and slightly unsettling in a way, but so unbelievably calming that it outweighed everything else. The soft, easy slide in and out was right and true and made me feel unimaginably complete.

Her body twitched, pulling me deeper still. My fingers stretched up her back, reaching under her hair to stroke the Eye on the back of her neck, and then I felt her body clench around me with the need to release.

"With me, Evelyn, always with me," I panted and groaned with bliss as my pumps became urgent and erratic. We were both teetering on the precipice of oblivion and couldn't wait to fall together.

Everything stopped for a second as every muscle in my body seized. The orgasm shook me to the very core, wrapping itself around Evelyn's climax and molding with it to ratchet them both into one massive crescendo that neither one of us had ever achieved before, even with each other.

We'd just made love in front of Lana and Isolde, we were bloody and spent, and yet it didn't feel seedy or perverse in any way. Not because we got off on people watching or anything like that, but because two people had witnessed another two people committing themselves to one another, and it had been the most beautiful thing I'd experienced in my short life.

As the energy in the room dissipated we lay on the floor together, and I became vaguely aware of movement outside of Evie and myself. The quiet puff of the candles going out, the warm wet cloths wiping the blood away, and the gentle fingers against my skin as healing balm was applied to the wounds on my back and palms.

When we could gather the strength and desire to move again, we donned our robes and picked up our swords. Silently, we made our way back up to our room, where we huddled under the sheet on our bed and held each other close for the remainder of the night.

We didn't speak or make love. We just…were. One, complete, whole.

CHAPTER 9
EVELYN

As morning reared its ugly head again, Daniel and I didn't want to move, let alone disengage our limbs from one another. We'd stayed entwined throughout the night because we knew what today would bring.

Separation.

Today I would be leaving the house, and we would be apart for who knew how long. I was going to be taking up residence with Lana, Maria, and Tess in a small house tucked between a local arts institute and community college, posing as students, which were Anabael's latest quarry.

Local art institute? That was a misnomer if I'd ever heard one. "Local" was twenty-some odd miles up the 405. I mean, it really wasn't far, but as anyone who had ever driven on the 405 could tell you, walking would have been faster. It didn't matter what time of day or even what day of the week it was, that damn stretch of freeway was always bumper to bumper. I fought for a closer location, UCLA or even the LA Art Institute, but Tony's research had found that Anabael preferred suburbia these days.

It made perfect sense. When you thought about it, someone falling off the map and disengaging from family in the big city wasn't unheard of. Hell, one could argue that it was half expected, especially among the college-age youth who were clamoring to become independent. But in a town like San Valencita, the kids at the local community college and art institute either rented a house with friends, while mommy and daddy helped pay the rent, or they continued to live at home. One way or the other, odds were that a good portion of them had parents who were desperate to hang on to their fading youth.

Most moms in that area were the textbook version of a "cougar" who spent the day drinking bottle after bottle of wine and shopping, all the while trolling their daughter's male friends looking for the one they could boink in the bathroom when no one was looking. That's who Anabael was really after in the long run, not the little feeder fish but the big bad shark they attached themselves to. Local doctors, lawyers, mayor and city council types—hell, this close to Hollywood, I'd have bet there was even a fair share of entertainment industry types that lived here. If she could get one prominent member of the community into her fold, she could practically have the entire town just on the keeping-up-with-the-Joneses factor; that's how most of these Stepford-like, middle and upper class suburban wastelands were.

So we would go in under the guise of four spoiled rich girls playing the "independent" game. I was the clincher, the cousin who had moved in from the East Coast and needed to make a little extra cash on the side, exactly what Beautiful Illuminations was looking for.

Daniel's arms tightened around me, and he made a little noise in the back of his throat that ripped my heart to shreds. My chest ached like my sternum had been punched in, and I had a hard time breathing.

"Shhh…" He stroked my hair. "I'll be fine. We'll be fine. You'll get that nasty bitch and be back here with me before you even realize you miss me, and then I'll remind you what you missed the most." He reached down and squeezed my ass cheek, making me chuckle.

"You're such a cheese ball."

Later while I packed, I fished a couple of Daniel's shirts out of the dirty laundry. Yeah, I know it sounds gross—okay, it *was* gross—but I had to have something of his that smelled like him, just had to.

The guys helped us pack up the car, a generic sedan. Not too showy and not too boring, perfect for blending in.

As we crawled up the freeway, I thought about Daniel. Shit, I already missed him like hell. I must have looked just as miserable as I felt, because Lana turned around in the front passenger seat.

"Do you want to know?" she asked.

"Know what?"

"If I see you coming back? I have not seen one way or the other and I might not, but if I do, do you want to know what I see?"

I thought about it for a moment. What if she saw that I didn't come back? Did I want to know that I'd just seen Daniel for the last time? Did I want to know that the last time he saw me would be whatever state of dead I came back in?

"No." I shook my head. "Probably not a good idea. It might throw me off my game, ya know?"

She looked at me, sadness in her eyes as if she could tell the real reason why I didn't want to know. "Yes, I understand."

"Ladies, here we are, home sweet home." Maria pressed the garage door opener and drove in. The house was within walking distance of the community college, situated next to an opulent gated community. It looked simple and cozy enough and blended into the other little matchbox houses we'd passed to get to it. Beige, completely and totally beige.

"Not bad, I guess, if you're into living in Generic Von Boringland," Tess muttered as we walked through the living room and headed toward the kitchen. "I hope this joint has a gas range. I have concoctions to cook up and hate working with those electric burners. Controlling the heat on those damn things can be an enormous bitch."

She was still nattering on as I started down the hall. On the way here, we'd discussed room assignments and decided that Tess and I would share the master bedroom. She hated to sleep alone, and according to her, I was the only one she could poop in front of. Well, wasn't I the lucky one.

"Gas stove and six burners, perfect," she announced as she followed me into the large room. "Drop your bags and vacate, girl. I need to drop a food baby. That breakfast burrito Chris made me this morning is rolling around in my gut like a shit demon."

"Nice. Thanks, T." Grabbing the assignment folder out of my shoulder bag, I got the hell out of there. Seriously, if we could harness the stench of Tess's shit bombs, we would have one deadly ass weapon on our hands.

Sitting at the dining room table, I cracked open the manila envelope. In addition to my fake ID, I had a fictitious class schedule.

In other words, for all intents and purposes, I was a student at San Valencita Community College, in case anyone went digging. There were also the deets on the local Beautiful Illuminations rep and where I was most likely to "accidentally" run into her, complete with a picture. Marissa Splonski—spiky blond hair, fake boobs, eight pounds of makeup, and an inordinate amount of bling. Have Bedazzler, Will Travel much? According to Tony's notes—and by "notes," I meant the stuff he'd found out when he hacked into their mainframe—the last few young ladies had been "recruited" at the market, a bar, and a Starbucks, and based on her track record, she liked to troll on Mondays and Fridays.

Perfect. Today was Wednesday, so we had a couple of days to get our bearings and for Tess to brew up some magic juice, a little extra boost to protect me from getting totally taken over if the Specs managed to get inside my head. And with the amount of grocery-type bags Tess had with her, this was gonna be a doozy.

Man alive, "doozy" didn't even begin to describe what was being done to me at the moment. I was sprawled out on the kitchen table, the rank smell of the shit Tess was cooking filling up the room. What was it about these potions? Couldn't at least one of them *not* smell like sweaty ass wrapped in old gym socks, and not taste just as bad?

Now she came at me with a bowl.

"What the hell is *that?*" I sat up on my elbows, trying to get a peek inside.

"Your special beauty mask, my dear. Take a whiff." She shoved the bowl up under my nose. "Great for the pores and sinuses and for protecting that warped little mind of yours. Once I slather you with this, whatever juju they use to get inside people's heads will bounce right off."

"Oh holy shit!" My eyes watered and the inside of my nostrils felt like they'd been literally singed by the stench. "Once, just once, can you at least try to make your potions smell good? There's got to be some kind of essential oils you can put in it to take the edge off."

"Sweetie, this *is* the good smelling stuff. Just wait until you get a load of what you get to drink later. Lie back; it's time for your facial."

With a groan, I flopped back onto the table and promptly cracked my noggin on the oak. "Can I at least get a pillow?"

Tess quirked her head at me and smiled big. "That, my darling, I can most definitely do." Ducking into the living room, she grabbed one of the throw pillows from the couch and tucked it under my head.

"Thanks, Mommy, that's nice," I teased as I settled back onto the plump velvet square. "Read me a story."

"Once upon a time, there was a hunter who stopped being a smart-ass long enough for her best friend to do her job so she didn't get her brain whammied when she went to meet up with the big bad she-demon skank whore."

I laughed until I heard Tess snap on a pair of rubber gloves.

"Really?"

"What? I'm not touching this shit. It smells like a dead goat. Now close your eyes and think happy thoughts."

The cold, slimy drag of Tess's goo-covered finger on my forehead made me shudder.

"Be still or I'm gonna fuck up the characters and have to start all over again."

Gripping the edges of the table, I anchored myself and forced my body not to move because God knew I didn't want to have to go through this any longer than necessary. With a low murmur, Tess continued drawing on my forehead...

Ptristmindo phecture peteik.

Over and over again, with every swipe of her finger.

Ptristmindo phecture peteik.

A warm sensation began under each marking, burrowing down into my brain.

Ptristmindo phecture peteik.

Further and further until it felt like a warm blanket was wrapped around my mind, cocooning it.

Later that night after I scrubbed my forehead raw trying to get rid of the smell and snot-like texture, I sat on the edge of the tub in the master bathroom and called Daniel.

"Must be six, 'cause I could set my clock to you, babe," he said when he picked up. "Not that I was sitting here with the phone in my hand watching the time or anything."

I had to laugh. Damn but we were a pathetic pair. Before I had left, we'd decided to call each other at six and six, at the very least, no matter what. So far we'd been apart for a day and a half and had talked to each other on the phone approximately twelve times. Granted, a few of those were just the *I miss you*s and *Me too*s, but yeah, we were pretty freaking pathetic.

"I miss you," I sighed, just happy to hear the sound of his voice.

"Me too," he purred. "I hate sleeping alone."

"Yeah, I'm stuck with Tess, and she kicks in her sleep. I don't know how Chris stands it. Speaking of Tess, she slathered smelly gunk on my head today and made me drink possibly the worst stuff she's made me drink in over a hundred years."

The rich sound of his laugher made the warm sensation in my head tingle.

"That's nothing. Isolde made me…" He stopped. "Um, shit, I can't tell you."

That was how a lot of conversations had gone in the last day and a half. I couldn't know what preparations were being made in the house. It was a safety precaution, in case a Spec got inside my head. We didn't want them to know what we had in store for them, so the less I knew the better.

"It's okay, I get it," I reassured him. "Hey, I finally get to go out trolling tomorrow. Wish me luck and that the fish are out and hungry."

"Good luck, and be careful."

"Always."

CHAPTER 10
DANIEL

After hanging up with Evie, I gripped my phone and resisted every urge in my body not to throw it across the room in frustration. I hated having to hide things from her like this, but Alex and Gabriel's instructions had been crystal clear. The meeting we'd had after she'd left the house came flooding back.

"Daniel," Gabriel said as he stood in front of me, hands pressed into the pockets of his Italian slacks, "now that Evelyn has taken leave of the house, we can focus on your assignment."

"What do you mean? I thought I was doing—am doing what you've asked of me."

"You are, Daniel. You are doing very well with the pieces of the mission we've handed to you thus far, but your true assignment is only beginning. We are going to ask some very difficult things of you, and I wish there was a better way to tell you this, but there simply is not."

I felt my eyes widen. Jiminy Christmas, what the hell else did they want from me?

"While Evelyn is away, it is imperative that you keep your activities within the home a secret. You cannot even hint at one single iota of information, do you understand?"

"Yeah, I thought we'd already established that, though, in case…ya know." God, I couldn't even say it.

"There is no 'in case,' Daniel. That is only what we wished Evelyn to believe. She absolutely had to believe that there was a chance —"

"Wait a second," I said. "What the hell are you saying?"

Alex sighed and pinched the bridge of his nose under his glasses. It looked like even he was having a hard time with this. "She's going to be taken, Daniel. You need to prepare yourself for that. We need to prepare you for it."

A laugh burst out of me. "You're fucking with me, right? I mean, you wouldn't have sent her out there alone believing that she had a hint of a chance to fight off this…this Spectoral thing." My voice grew louder and angrier with every word that flew out of my mouth. When neither one of them spoke up to deny my accusation, I blew.

"You sent her off to fight the wolves with nothing but a plastic spork and a healthy dose of false hope!"

"No, she is armed with the knowledge of over a hundred years of demon battle, backed by a psychic hunter and a handler trained in magic by the best theurgist in the company," Gabriel stated with such force that it took me aback. "Surely you do not believe that we would send her on assignment completely exposed. However, Anabael's powers are mighty, and she will overtake Evelyn and possess her. Make no mistake, that is going to happen."

I sank to the chair; what little comfort I'd gathered from Gabriel's first statement had shriveled at the second. Gabriel squatted to the floor directly in front of me, putting himself in my line of sight.

"Do not despair, child. You need to remain strong and hopeful. Evelyn will need every ounce you can spare if she is going to come back to us."

Nodding, I took a long, deep breath and straightened my spine. "Okay, what do I need to do?"

"Brilliant." Alex smiled. "Now, as Gabriel mentioned, Evelyn has been made aware that possession is a possibility and that she has physical forms of backup for her protection. Also, upon arrival at her destination, she will be imbued with supernatural assistance to keep her mind clear and her soul intact. However, I want to be very clear: Evelyn is an integral part of this family. She is the closest thing Isolde and I have to an actual daughter. Losing her is not an option." The depth of determination in Alex's voice helped calm my unease. "Now follow me, as you will need a new marking."

He swung the door to his office open, and I followed him and Gabriel up the stairs. After passing through the kitchen, we turned into a room I'd never been in before, an office just off the formal dining room. The space was immaculately clean but had an innately comforting feel to it.

Isolde stood over by the window in the corner, hovering over a chair draped with a cloth. As she stepped away to greet us, I saw that there was an interesting array of items on the tall table next to the window: clippers, a long stick with a pointy end, and a razor. I watched as Gabriel produced a small clay pot out of thin air. He held it in the palm of his hand and closed his eyes. His lips moved around words I couldn't hear, and the little ancient jar glowed purple and vibrated for a moment before he handed it over to Isolde. After she set down the clay pot, she picked up the clippers and razor and walked toward me.

"What I am about to mark you with is very sacred: The Path of Aurora. It will allow you to reach Evelyn in her darkest hour. Theoretically, it could be placed anywhere on the body, but it is most effective when it is placed on the highest point," Isolde explained as she glanced at the top of my head.

My hand went up to my hair automatically, remembering all the times Evs had said how much she loved it. She liked playing with it when we were lying in bed, wrapping it around her fingers and pulling it deliciously when we made love.

"I know it seems extreme, but this charm may be the only thing that saves her life. It saved mine." Isolde looked at Alex with a warm smile. He bowed his head and parted the hair at the top of his head, the purple tattoo peeking out from his scalp.

"Not that it matters—it's happening whether it's etched on with acid or licked on by puppies—I'd just like to be prepared. Did it hurt?" I asked Alex.

"Like the devil."

"Incidentally, there is a modicum of Lucifer's essence in the ink," Gabriel said. "The presence of it should allow you to reach through Anabael's hold on Evelyn."

"Okay, let's do this thing."

Alex led me to another chair on the other side of the room and motioned for me to sit as Isolde wrapped a long plastic cape around my neck. I closed my eyes as I heard the electric clippers buzz to life and sucked in a breath when I felt the metal teeth touch my scalp. I don't know what

I'd expected, a pulling sensation maybe, but all I felt was an odd vibration against my noggin and the soft whoosh of the hair sliding down the plastic cape and into my lap. Clumps of hair tickled down the back of my neck as I found myself absorbing the drone of the clippers, a sound I found oddly comforting as it was reminiscent of the purr of Evie's tattoo gun. When I opened my eyes for a moment, I saw that the sunlight streaming through the window behind me had cast my silhouette in the glass of one of the pictures across the room—one of Evie that looked to have been taken sometime in the early nineteen hundreds. She looked as beautiful then as she did now, and it made me miss her even more.

I closed my eyes again, trying to lose myself in the sensations happening now. The clippers were off and a warm, wet towel was being wrapped around my head. After a few minutes it was removed, and I felt what I imagined to be some sort of shaving lotion being rubbed all over the surface of my melon. The distinct scrape of a razor gliding over my skin brought back more thoughts of Evie. She always shaved a patch of skin before she tattooed it.

"Daniel."

The sound of Isolde's voice popped my eyes open, and I saw her pat the chair next to the table I'd seen before. The clay pot was open now; the cork stopper lay next to it, and small curls of lavender smoke plumed out from the top.

"I wish I could use the machine to mark you, but this particular charm must be pushed into the skin the old-fashioned way." She picked up the old stick and dipped the pointy end into it, leaving it covered in a deep plum-colored, glowing ink.

My throat swallowed so much air that I had to quietly let out a burp. I sat down in the chair and Alex handed me a rubber bite block.

"I'm okay," I said, waving it away and gripping the arms of the chair.

He cocked his eyebrow. "Take it, trust me."

Reluctantly, I placed the hunk of rubber in my mouth and prepared myself for the first poke. I took a deep breath in through my nose, and when I started to exhale around the bit in my mouth, I felt the first stab. My teeth clenched down so hard I was surprised I didn't bite the damned thing in half. God, it felt like a red-hot poker dipped in lemon juice jabbing into the back of my head. Again and again, pain lanced through my brain so white hot and intense I thought my brain would melt. Then I realized that Isolde was chanting…

Giblaun igthto dor'kraetha.

She kept repeating the same phrase, as if pushing the words into my skull with every dig of the needle.

When I thought I couldn't bear another moment of this agony, she stopped. "We are finished for today," she said, setting the stick down on the table next to the ink jar.

My head felt like it was on fire, the agony so all-consuming I could barely gather up the strength to remove the rubber bite guard from my mouth. But Gabriel took my hand in one of his, and as he passed the palm of his other hand over my scalp, the pain melted almost instantaneously.

"Why didn't we just keep going and get this bad boy tapped out right here and now?" I asked him.

"Because, while I have taken away the pain, you need some time to absorb this ink. Too much of it at once would overwhelm your young human body. Not to mention it takes its toll on our Isolde as well, working this kind of magic. She will finish tomorrow. Go back to your room and rest."

That had been two days ago. The day after that, Isolde did finish the charm, and I now sported a bright purple ink Mohawk in addition to a wealth of ancient symbols. Intertwined between the patterns was the inscription of the incantation of the Path of Aurora and Evie's name, Evelyn. Every single speck of skin had been claimed in her honor.

I ran my hand over the top of my head. It felt weird as hell not to have hair, and it was surprisingly cold; I'd even taken to running around the house in one of those ridiculous hipster beanies.

It was hard not to tell Evie about it all, but if it meant her safety, I'd bite the end of my tongue off before I divulged anything. Telling her I loved her and to be safe would have to suffice for now.

CHAPTER 11
EVELYN

Granted, I'd never gone fishing for actual fish, but if I were a betting woman, I'd bet that fishing for demons followed the same three simple rules:

One, know where they were biting. In this case, the watering hole of choice was the grocery store closest to the community college, the very one that a couple of girls had been recruited from in recent months.

Two, use the proper bait. Based on the channel and time when Beautiful Illuminations ran their paid-for television ads, the target audience was the younger generation. If I had to guess, Anabael had a good portion of the local cougar-mom set buying into her "for women by women" crap and now she was gunning for the daughters. Cue college chic, baggy might-be-pajama pants, old T-shirt, hoodie, and a cart full of party necessities: chips, an assortment of dips, and of course beer and other sorts of liquor.

And the most important component of all, a big ol' helping of patience.

"Oh, grab some of those toaster breakfast things. Not the fruity ones but the pastries with sausage and stuff in 'em," Tess squawked in my earpiece as I pushed my cart down the freezer aisle.

"Fine, but then I think we need to call it for this store and maybe try another one. I've been here for over an hour, and the staff is starting to look at me weird."

"Good call, but bring the food back first. I'm jonesing for one of those toaster things."

As I opened the glass door and reached into the frozen-food case, the hairs on the back of my neck sprang straight up. There was only one thing that did that to me—a demon. With a sly glance to the side, I saw a well-manicured hand reach into the case next to me. Okay, time to get my act on.

Picking up the box of frozen breakfast pastries, I made a good show of looking at the yellow price tag hanging off the shelf, then over to the items already in my cart and back again. I flicked the tag with my finger and tapped the box like I was trying to decide if I could afford it or not. One quick look into my purse to count the money in my wallet should convey that I was struggling with funds. And finally, with a heavy sigh, I put the box back on the shelf and started to walk away.

As I turned in her direction, she made eye contact and smiled.

Got a nibble.

"I used to go to my parents' house and stock up from their freezer," she said with a wink and straightened to her full height. Crap, she was tall.

"I wish," I said with another sigh.

"So who's the hard-ass, Mom or Dad?"

"Mom," I sneered. "Well, actually my new stepdad. He's all, 'If she wants to play the adult game and live on her own, she needs to be completely on her own.' Which is fine. She thinks the world revolves around him and his fancy new dick anyway. Oh my God, I can't believe I just told you that. I don't even know you. I'm so sorry, I guess I just needed to vent that."

"No worries, honey. It does explain some things, though." She nodded to the beer and whiskey in my shopping cart.

"Riiight?"

"Seriously, though, please tell me that's not all for you. I couldn't in good conscience let you walk away if you intend to consume all of that on your own." She looked at me with what appeared to be genuine concern.

"What? Oh, no, not even. My roommates and I are having a party tonight, and it's just not a party without our favorite guys, Bud and Jack."

"Ahh, yes, I remember those party days. What if I told you that you could not only get paid to have parties but that you could use your 'party supplies' as tax write-offs?"

SCORE!

"I'd say hells yeah, where do I sign up?" I couldn't make it too easy for her, though; that would be too obvious. I narrowed my eyes. "But come on, seriously, is this for reals? You aren't trying to, like, ya know, lure me into some kind of slave trade thing like you see in the movies, because I heard those were, like, for reals."

Digging in her Louis Vuitton handbag, she pulled out a lavender business card that vaguely smelled like old-lady perfume and waved it at me. It made my nose tingle in a strange way that made my hunter instincts scream. Something was up with this scent or maybe even the paper itself.

"No, nothing like that. This is totally legit. My name is Marissa, sweetie, and I was stuck in a bad marriage. Beautiful Illuminations gave me the start I needed to take control of my life. I just wish I had gotten that start when I was your age. Show your mom and stepdad you *can* do this on your own. Take charge of your future because, before you know it, you'll be stuck in a future that you don't want."

Damn, if I didn't know this was a load of horseshit, I might have actually bought into it.

"What do I have to do?"

"Don't worry about it right now. You have a party to get ready for." She nodded to my cart again and winked. "Call me tomorrow. I've got one hell of a hangover cure that you'll want to share with all of your friends."

She walked away, the clicking of her heels against the linoleum reverberating off of the giant freezers.

Fish hooked. Now all I need to do is reel the bitch in.

Feigning a hangover the next afternoon wasn't a big issue. Lana had seen something up with the business card, and after staying up all night with Tess testing it, I felt like I really had downed that bottle of Jack.

Sure as shit, that bad boy was laced with *helvista*, an herb that was prevalent in the third level of Hell and made a person more inclined to agree to anything. Demons often used it on innocents because it couldn't be traced in any sort of test—unless you were a hunter or handler and knew what to look for.

Hunched over a table in the little courtyard between Starbucks and Jamba Juice, I pushed my aviators up my nose and pretended that I didn't see Marissa walking toward me. She was kind of hard to miss, though, with that platinum blond hair that stood on end, giant boobs that didn't bounce in the slightest, and makeup that *had* to have been put on with a trowel.

"Up at the crack of noon. I remember when I could sleep like that," she sang as she slid into the chair across from mine.

I groaned. "You said something about magic hangover juice."

"Of course." She pulled a plastic drink container out of her giant bag. Its contents looked like barf. Scratch that—it looked worse than barf, like something Tess would make me drink.

"Jesus, what the hell is in that?"

"Oh ya know, eye of newt, tongue of dog, the blood of five virgins, that kind of thing."

I cocked my eyebrow over the rim of my sunglasses, and she laughed uproariously.

"I'm kidding, of course." She smiled at me, so sickeningly sweetly that I had the creepy feeling that she wasn't kidding in the least. "It's just all-natural herbs and proteins to balance your system out, one of our Beautiful Illuminations best sellers. Try it; it isn't as bad as it looks."

She popped the little cup top off and turned it upside down. As she opened the container and poured, the distinct smell of *helvista* assaulted my nostrils. If that wasn't bad enough, I was pretty sure I could detect the scent of blood, too.

Holy shit. My stomach lurched of its own accord, and I had to put my fist to my mouth to hold back the urge to hurl.

"Do not vomit," Lana's voice sounded in my earpiece. She was seated on the other end of the courtyard as my backup, watching everything go down. It was weird; being this close to her, I should have been getting clear reception, but Lana sounded like she was inside a trashcan. "This is what we expected, and the potion Tessa made for you this morning will encapsulate the liquid and hold it. I told you, you must drink to gain her trust, but you will remain unharmed, I assure you."

Wrapping my fingers around the little plastic cup, I raised it in salute before swilling it down like a shot of tequila. Miraculously, I didn't taste a thing, but I could feel the liquid slither down my throat and plop into my gut.

"So, listen," Marissa began as I put the cup down. "I'm having an introductory meeting at my house tomorrow at four. There'll be food, an open bar, and I want you to come. You can even bring your roommates if they're interested. No obligations, just come and see what Beautiful Illuminations is all about."

"You had *me* at open bar. I'll talk to my roommates, but Tara is in the middle of some nasty guy issue, Lindsay is a flake, and Mary, well, she's just an outright bitch."

"That's fine, you are more than enough." She placed a hand on mine and gave it a squeeze. "So, I'll see you tomorrow, and trust me, you'll absolutely love it. I can just feel it."

Yeah, I could feel it, too—I felt that stuff I'd drank rolling around in my gut like it was alive. Thankfully, there wasn't much left of the meeting. Marissa gave me her address just before she skipped off into the sunset. Lana, thank God, was right there as soon as Marissa ducked out of sight. She practically had to help me to the car because it was taking all my effort not to upchuck until I got home. And I had to wait so that Lana and Maria could analyze my stomach contents.

Using every ounce of self-control I could call upon, I staggered into the house and practically ripped the big mixing bowl out of Maria's hands. Sinking into one of the kitchen chairs, I unclenched my insides and tried to relax. Not as easy as it sounded. I could feel my body working to regurgitate, the muscles pulling and twisting as that putrid swill rose to my throat. I opened my mouth over the bowl and watched in shock as I coughed over and over again and basically gave oral birth to a sack of goop. When it finally landed in the bowl, the contents sloshing inside of an opaque bubble, I sat back and wiped at the sweat pouring down my face.

"That was the freakiest shit I've ever seen in my entire life," Tess said, staring into the bowl.

"You're telling me." I wheezed and shuddered, my voice sounding like I'd just gargled nails. "Just FYI, I am *never* doing that ever again."

Lana and Maria went to work analyzing Marissa's special hangover juice. Thank God and all of his creations I hadn't actually ingested that crap, because not only was it loaded to the gills with *helvista*, it was packed with another little bit of herbal mess from the Hell plane, *morguancha*. Those two were typically found in a concoction together. The *helvista* made you agreeable to do pretty much anything, and *morguancha* compelled you to carry out what you'd just agreed to. On top of that, it was chock full of human hemoglobin, which when mixed with the other two components was like signing a contract in blood. And unbeknownst to the average human, a blood contract didn't necessarily have to be signed with your own.

Ugh. The thought of it made me want to puke all over again, and I used a whole tube of toothpaste scrubbing my entire mouth. Honestly, if I could have reached down my throat and given the inside of my stomach and esophagus a good disinfecting, I would have. Man alive, the people who actually drank that crap didn't have a chance in hell of saying no to Beautiful Illuminations' offer.

Standing in front of Marissa's house, I patted my bag for the bugs I'd be planting and adjusted my earpiece to make sure it was hidden. Daniel had wanted to use a spell we'd done before that allowed us to hear each other's thoughts, but that wasn't an option this time. For one, it only worked for two people, and those two people had to be within close proximity of one another, not miles apart like we were now.

I looked at my reflection in the car window and straightened the camera hidden in the button on my blouse so the guys back at home could see what was going on.

"Damn, I miss your boobs," Daniel said over the earpiece. It was nice to hear his voice in my head again. It almost felt like he was there with me even though he was all the way over at the mansion. Normally Tess, Lana, and Maria would be watching and listening from the small house nearby, but they were already here, casing the outside, while I was working the people on the inside. So we needed Daniel to monitor our movement and be our connection to each other. He could see where the others were via Tony hacking into a satellite feed, and he could see where I was in the house through my button cam. If my girls were busy listening to me instead, they couldn't concentrate on their part of the mission, so it was up to Daniel to keep them apprised of any danger I might find myself in so they could swoop in and vice versa.

"My boobs miss you, too. Now quit ogling my rack and focus."

"Don't drink the Kool-Aid," he warned.

As I started up the walkway toward Marissa's house, I noted that everything was immaculate. The grass had been cut down to the perfect length, bushes and flowerbeds meticulously trimmed and weeded; hell, I'd have bet that if a stray leaf happened to float down, it would be vaporized before it could land anywhere. The exterior of the house looked just as flawless, painted in coordinating shades of—what else—*beige* and looked like it could have been on the cover of *Better Homes and Gardens*.

I raised my hand to knock on the door and was half startled when it swung open. Marissa stood in the doorway with the biggest wine glass I'd ever seen.

"You made it," she said with a squeal and pulled me into a hug that felt like she was trying to crush my bones.

"Yeah, can't breathe." I grunted, stiffening in her grasp. My hunter instinct was to lash out and pin the overgrown Barbie of a beast to the wall, but I had to maintain my cover.

"Sorry, love." She released me and ushered me inside. "I get a little excited bringing new people into the wonderful world of Beautiful Illuminations. Come and meet my team. I've told them all about you, and they can't wait."

Rounding the corner, the room was filled with a good fifty-fifty mix of actual humans and Specs in human skin. So that was how they managed to keep such a low profile and Beautiful Illuminations off of Lebriga's map—not everyone involved had been possessed.

"Wow, you have a beautiful home," I said as I scanned the place, looking for where I might be able to plant a bug. "Your ex-husband must have gotten completely shafted."

"Yes, well, he would have if he had made it through the divorce. Such a shame. He had a brain aneurism in the garage on the way to meet his lawyer."

Brain aneurism, my ass.

"But enough about that. Someone get my girl Erin a glass of wine."

Erin was the name I'd given to her, my go-to alias. Before I could politely decline, a glass was shoved into my hand and I was being hauled around the room and introduced to everyone individually. Every single one of them pulled me into a hug, squeezing me like an orange as they squealed their excitement in my ear. I really needed to get away and plant some bugs and get the hell out of there before they crushed me to death. Plus, one of those God-awful screeches must have messed with my earwig; I could only hear static.

"It really is nice to meet everyone, but I had a Trenta from Starbucks on my way over here, and if I get squeezed again, I'm going to pee everywhere."

The entire room erupted with giggles, and Marissa pointed out the way to the restroom. As soon as I was out of everyone's sight, I took off down the hall, moving with soundless speed. I wasn't sure how much time I had to work with, but these bugs needed to be planted.

Wiggling my finger in my ear, I jostled the mechanism around. "Daniel?"

"Evs, can you hear me?" he asked.

"Kind of. I think there's something wrong with this receiver. You sound like you're in a tunnel."

"Same on my end. This isn't safe. Alex says to plant the bugs and get the hell out of there."

Ducking into the master bedroom, I stuck a receiver on the ceiling next to the light fixture and one in the bathroom at the top of the mirror. Thanks to Tony and his handler Walter's tech magic, not only did these bugs transmit audio and video, but the surface of them also morphed into whatever they were fixed to and became all but invisible.

Next was what looked to be an office, and I slapped a bug in there by the door so we could get a shot of the entire room. Moving along, I was able to set at least one receiver in every bedroom and one in the hall and entryway. The only places left to do were the rooms that had people in them.

Popping inside of the bathroom, I flushed the toilet, just in case someone had come looking for me.

Back in the room with everyone else, I did everything I could to avoid eating or drinking anything. After finding out what Marissa had put in that hangover cure, I wasn't about to put even a crumb in my mouth. As I listened to her and all her cronies nattering on and on about the wonders of Beautiful Illuminations, I could see where one might be tempted to drink the infamous Kool-Aid. Of course, the average person didn't know that they ran the risk of ending up as a Spec flesh suit.

"So, what do you think so far?" Marissa asked. "Come to one of our beautification parties. I have one set up on Wednesday night. You can come and watch me work my magic."

"I don't know." I hemmed and hawed, trying to buy myself some time because all kinds of hunter alarms were going off. I had a feeling that "working her magic" was in the literal sense and that by the end of all the beautification bullshit, I'd be singing Beautiful Illuminations' praises. And the stupid-ass jingle from their commercial. Nope, I liked to be the one in control of my brain function, thanks.

"That's too bad. There's a big BI sales meeting at Corporate on Friday, and Annabelle Simmons herself is going to be onsite to give a presentation. These meetings are so amazing. You come away from them so filled with the Beautiful Illuminations spirit, and Annabelle is the epitome of feminine wisdom. The only problem is that you have to be enrolled as a beautification specialist by Wednesday at the latest to attend."

Hello there, Interest; meet Piqued. Annabelle Simmons had to be Anabael of Simzahnomon, so this could be the ticket in I was looking for. What better place to get at the head of the snake but in its nest. If I could get into Corporate, I could bring down Anabael from within. Something in my gut was pinging, but this was a shot I couldn't miss. Now if I could just worm my way out of that stupid beautification party—the last thing I needed was to have my head cooked before I even got to the big barbeque.

"Wow, that sounds like a great opportunity, but I have class on Wednesday night. Do I really have to do the beautification party part?"

"I'm sorry, hon', it's policy. Do you have any friends in class who can take notes for you? I would really hate for you to miss this. Meeting Annabelle alone is a once-in-a-lifetime opportunity."

"Well, when you put it that way, how can I say no?" I took a deep breath and screwed on my best cheerleader smile. "I'm in!" I threw my hands in the air for good measure.

A huge, slightly malevolent smile spread across Marissa's face.

"Now I *know* you're a perfect fit for BI." Her voice was cooler than before, almost sinister. Only a hint, though, a glimpse of the Spectoral demon rolling around inside of her skin before she snapped back to her overly happy, probably-used-to-be-a-cheerleader self. "Oh, you will absolutely love both the beautification party and the sales meeting. You know, we call it a 'sales meeting,' but really it's just a giant party. Imagine the biggest girls' night you've ever been to, times a thousand. It will absolutely be the most amazing night of your life. You'll feel like a whole new person."

Yeah, I'll bet.

"Cool, I can't wait!" The soft whir of static in my ear made me itchy. I needed to get out of here, now. "Look, Mariss, I hate to bale so early in the night, but I got a text from my friend while I was in the bathroom. She's all strung out on some guy who's being a complete dillhole."

"Oh, honey, we've all been there. Am I right, girls?" she asked the room, and they all nodded emphatically. "I can pick you up on Wednesday night for the beautification party if you want. How's seven sound?"

"You know what, I have a late afternoon lab, so I'll probably come right from school. Can you give me the address, and I'll meet you there at seven?"

"Of course, doll. Anything to get you to that party. See you Wednesday." She looked at me strangely, like she knew I was lying. No, it was like she knew who I really was. Nah, there was no way she could possibly know; all the static in my head was making me feel extra sketchy.

As soon as I was out and the door closed behind me, the sound of Daniel's voice crackled over my earpiece.

"Something's wrong. Lana is going into seizures."

CHAPTER 12
DANIEL

"Where are they?" Evie asked. I could see through the image from her button cam that she was walking toward her car—and walking fast, trying not to run.

"I got it," Tony said as he tapped out a code on the keyboard, and boom, the image before me changed from the one from Ev's button cam to the satellite feed. The picture zoomed out, and before I could ask him to do it, he had the fastest route highlighted.

"Okay, head to the pickup site on the next block," I instructed. "They should be there. Hurry, but don't draw attention to yourself. You're still undercover."

"I know how to do my job, Daniel," she barked. Wow, that seemed to come through loud and clear. "Sorry," she said quietly as she punched the car into gear. Ev didn't apologize easily.

"Don't worry about it." I chuckled, trying to let her know that I didn't take the harsh words personally, because I didn't. She was under a lot of pressure. "Look, you focus on driving. I'll call you later tonight."

Tony and I watched to make sure the pickup went without any hitches. Once the other girls were safe in the car, we both sat back and breathed a sigh of relief.

That was hairy, to say the least. The second the door had opened to that Marissa's house, the image feed was like looking through a snowstorm and the audio hadn't been much better. Alex had all but had to order me to stay where I was, because having Evelyn in that den, for lack of a better term, had me freaked the hell out.

"Are you okay?" Tony asked behind me.

"Yeah." I scrubbed my hands over my face and shook my head, trying to shake out the freak-out. It didn't work so well, and I snapped. "Actually, no, there isn't a part of this assignment that is 'okay,' not even a little bit. But I don't have much choice, do I? I have to be okay. Ev needs me to be okay."

I immediately felt bad for lashing out at Tony. I pulled my hat off and rubbed at the purple markings on my head. They were slightly raised, different from the other tattoos on other parts of my body. They felt weird, but at the same time they felt right, like they belonged there.

"That's some next-level shit. You know that, right?" Tony nodded to my head. "That…damn, I don't have words. That's some serious commitment, man."

"What do you mean? You'd do it for Josie, wouldn't you?"

"Yeah, but we've also been together since the fifties. You and Evie have only been together for what, less than a year?"

"Nah." I shook my head. "I think we've always been together, ya know?"

"No, I don't know," he said, laughing. "Dude, she's over a hundred years older than you are. How have you always been together? Wait, were you a virgin? Did you save your little hunter cherry for Ev to pluck?"

"What? No! Jesus, forget it."

"Come on, man, I'm just messing with ya. Seriously, though, how do you explain the whole age-difference thing?"

I took a deep breath and tried to put into words something that there wasn't any words for. How do you explain a color to a person who was born blind or a sound to someone who's never heard one?

"For as long as I can remember, I knew I was different than other kids. It's something we all experience before we become hunters, right? The weird kids who still slept with the lights on even though we were in high school, because we knew what was lurking in the dark and we were terrified. You saw it, we all did. In your neighbors, in your teachers, in the creepy bus driver who always gave you the stink eye. It was something you just knew, right?"

When Tony nodded, I continued. "But you tried to be normal, didn't you? I did. I tried like hell to be normal. I damn near had my entire life planned out. House in the suburbs, hot wife, three kids running around, that kind of stuff. But something was always off and I couldn't get out of my own way to let that happen."

I thought back to Meagan. I could have had all of that with her and damn near did. We had talked about it our senior year of high school. How we'd both go to the same college and after graduation have the big wedding with all the bells and whistles. We'd even started saving to buy a house on the same block as our parents. It should have been right, an easy choice, the perfect fairy tale. The problem was that the more we'd talked about and planned our lives, the more I'd felt like I was making all of the wrong choices. I couldn't see myself growing old with her; I could only see a life of monotonous misery, and I hadn't known why. I knew I loved her, on some level. Not enough to be all she needed but enough to let her go so she could find that life with someone else. Only she hadn't.

"Instead I chose being with girls that I knew weren't the right ones so I could easily slip out of commitment with them. I even tried being with a female hunter before I came here, thinking that maybe all the others weren't right because I wasn't with my 'kind' or whatever, but it still left me feeling…empty. Like when you eat something just to fill the void in your stomach. You're full but not satisfied because you really wanted chocolate cake and all you had to eat was celery.

"Then I saw Ev and shit started falling into place. And when we were finally together, it was like hallelujah, *this* is what I've been waiting for. I finally got my cake, and I ate the hell out of it. This woman was put on this planet for me, and I have lived for this woman all my life without even knowing what I was living for."

"Wow, that's incredible, man." Tony stood and placed a hand on my shoulder. "So did they install your vagina when they gave you the head tat, or was that extra?"

"Fuck you, asshole." I shoved his hand away and stormed out of the tech lab to the sound of his cackle.

"Don't let Anthony's ribald manner fool you," Alex said from the door of his office. "I assure you, he knows precisely what you mean, as do I." He stepped back as he gestured me inside.

"What's up?" I asked.

"I wanted to keep you informed as to the particulars of the assignment, and in doing so, you should know that we did not foresee Lana's episode. Anabael's forces are stronger than we had anticipated, and we believe that she somehow knows of our plans."

"Okay, so now what? We call the girls back in and we head back to the drawing board?"

"No, after discussing the situation with Gabriel, we have decided that we will maintain our course."

I blinked at him, dumbfounded by what I'd just heard. "I'm sorry, did you just say we're not calling Ev and the girls back?"

"That is correct."

"So, the perilous and highly unstable situation Evie is already in just got worse, and our plan of action is to do absolutely nothing?"

"I never said we weren't doing anything, I said we are staying the course. However, as Evelyn might say, this isn't our first time at the rodeo. Yes, the game has indeed changed. Therefore, we have implemented our own secret weapon."

CHAPTER 13
EVELYN

Trying not to drive like a bat out of hell, I pulled out into the main drive and rounded the corner onto the next block. I spotted them right away—Tess and Maria were walking down the street, essentially holding Lana up between them.

I quickly pulled over, jumped out, and flung open the back door. Maria got in first as Tess and I helped slide Lana in. Just as I was extracting myself from the rear seat, Lana gripped my wrist. Her eyes were wide, their blue irises almost completely eaten up by the black pupils.

"Did you say yes?" she asked, her accent thicker than it had ever been. I could barely understand her.

"What?"

"Did you say *yes?*" she shouted, sitting up, gripping my wrist with immense strength and shaking my entire arm so hard my teeth rattled. "They asked you to join them. Did you say yes?"

"Yeah, but—"

Her hand went slack, dropping from mine, and she sank back into Maria's lap, passed out.

I wanted to know what had happened, but I knew that we had to get back to the safety of the little house before I could ask any more questions. By the time we parked in the garage and shut the door behind us, Lana was still out cold. We carried her up to her room, and Maria took vigil by the side of her bed while Tess and I crowded in.

"What happened out there?" I finally asked.

"We had just finished the taps, setting up the outside receivers, when all of a sudden she shouted your name and began to convulse. It's not uncommon for her to seize with a vision, especially a strong one, but this was nuts."

Lana bolted straight up and stared at me. No, more like *through* me.

"There is a building…the street is empty, no traffic, no people, only a railway track…chain link fences…and buildings, warehouse buildings…factories…" Her voice faded off and her focus returned to me. "You are there, in front of a building…but I cannot…I cannot see what happens."

"It's okay," I said.

"No, it is not. I have tried to look further, but every time I try…" She shook her head. "If Isolde were here—"

The doorbell rang.

"Do you think…?" Tess cocked her eyebrow.

"It can't be," I said. "Izzy never leaves the house. I'll check it out."

As I headed downstairs to answer the door, I heard the lock snick and the door squeak open. With a flick of my wrist, I palmed the dagger I kept strapped to my thigh.

"Evelyn, I would appreciate it if you put your weapon away. I don't fancy being stabbed today," a voice called from around the corner.

"Isolde?"

"Perhaps I should have called first," she said, peeking around the wall and up the stairway. "And I do leave the house when the occasion calls for it," she added as she swished past me and into Lana's room.

"Damn, it's spooky when you do that," I muttered and followed her.

The moment Lana saw Isolde, you could almost feel the tension in her body release. She must have been really pent up, because she began to tremble all over.

"Shhh…" Isolde sat on the bed behind Lana, placing a hand on her back. "Rest, my child. We are all safe. Whatever is to come will not come on this day, so rest your mind and be at peace."

Lana closed her eyes and laid her head in Maria's lap while Isolde stroked the back of her hair.

In the days that followed Lana's episode, she and Isolde tried like hell to tap into that vision of hers, but their psychic connection seemed to short out as soon as they saw me standing in front of a warehouse. We weren't having much luck with our surveillance system either. After being in place for twenty-four hours, we should have had something to go on, but so far we didn't have dick.

"What in the hell did you do to those bugs, Ev?" Tony, tech genius extraordinaire, demanded over the phone. "Those were specially made, my top-of-the-line pieces. We're talking shit that the CIA *wishes* they could get their hands on. I should be getting crystal clear images, but the feed looks like some janky-ass nanny cam POS from Radio Shack."

"I didn't do anything to your damn bugs, Tony," I shot back into the receiver. "Look, I don't know what the problem is. All I know is that every time I've been around Marissa or her pack of fluffed up she-beasts, my earpiece goes wonky."

"Really, that's interesting," he said, and I could just picture him making that goofy duck face he made when he thought hard. "They always say on those ghost hunter shows that their instruments don't function properly when a spirit is around. I wonder if Spectorals have the same effect because they lack a corporeal base."

"Seriously, a ghost hunter show? That's where you're getting your intel? You really need to reevaluate your junk television habits, Tony. I'm starting to worry." I stopped for a second, though, and really thought about what he'd just said. "But then again, I guess it kinda makes sense. Could be why Lana is having a hard time latching on to a vision, too, even with Isolde's help."

"See, I told you one day my adoration for questionable reality TV would come in handy."

After I'd gotten off the phone with Tony, I had to get ready for that stupid beautification party thing. God, I did not want to do this, but I didn't have much of a choice.

Any kind of surveillance equipment was out, so Tess and Maria tailed me in Isolde's car as I met Marissa at a Starbucks around the corner from the party to go over some procedures beforehand.

The first thing Marissa whipped out was this funky makeup tool belt thing. Good Lord, Josie would probably have some sort of girly fit over this thing. It was stuffed to the gills with brushes, individually wrapped Q-tips, spongy circles, tissues, and to top it all, the fucking thing was sparkly pink leopard print. I had to quell the urge to throw up all over it.

"Oh, I almost forgot," Marissa said as she dug around in that giant purse of hers and pulled out a package wrapped in, guess what, pink leopard print paper. "Open it," she said with a squeal as she bounced in her seat.

Holding my stupid smile so hard my face was starting to ache, I unwrapped the paper and uncovered a gold lamé blouse with my fake name stitched on the front, just like the one Marissa herself wore.

"Wow, I don't know what to say," I said, doing my damnedest to sound sincere.

"You don't need to say anything, silly. You have just enough time to go change in the restroom before we go."

Passing the table that Tess and Maria were perched at, I slipped into the restroom, pulled my shirt off and buttoned up the hideous gold beast.

The door opened and Tess popped inside. She sidled up next to me and started to wash her hands. "That is a fabulous look. You need to keep that sucker after the assignment is over."

"Shut up, asshole," I grumbled.

"I love you, too," she said as I left and headed back to Marissa.

"Oh my goodness, just look at you!" Marissa exclaimed when I made it back to the table, and then we headed out to the parking lot. "One more thing, but I had to wait until we got outside to do this," she said once we reached her car. "Lean over."

"Excuse me?"

"Bend over."

As I did, I heard her digging around in that damned purse again; God only knew what she was going to pull out of it this time. The next thing I knew, her fingers were in my hair doing that fluff thing that Josie always did and I was being asphyxiated by a cloud of what I hoped was hairspray.

"And up," she instructed, maneuvering pieces of my hair into place and giving it one final coat of shellac. "Perfect!"

Looking at my reflection in the tinted car window, I saw that my hair was now twice its volume — and Tess, laughing so hard in the distance I'm surprised she didn't blow our cover altogether. Yes. Absolutely, positively, perfect.

"You look nervous," Marissa said to me as we neared our party location. *No, that would be the look of complete revulsion.* "Don't worry, I'll do all the talking. I just want you to observe and then just let it happen."

Let it happen? What the shit did that mean?

"Um, let what happen, exactly?"

"You'll see," she sang as she pulled into a driveway. "You're going to come out of this a newer, better woman."

Getting out of the car, I checked over my shoulder to make sure my backup team knew where I was. I had a panic button that I could use if I found myself in a sticky situation.

I should have pushed the damn thing when I realized what I had to "let happen": sitting in some lady's front room on one of her wooden dining room chairs, clutching the seat while Marissa slathered me with more makeup than I'd ever worn in my life.

Collectively.

Thank God Tess and Isolde had given me a protective facial before I'd left because who knew what was in this crap.

"Behold the transformation!" she declared as she shoved brushes back into her tool belt from hell. "This young woman came in here looking tired, worn out, and blah, ladies. Let's call a spade a spade — she was average."

My eyebrow cocked up, and I had to force it back down.

"But now look at her. What do you see? You see a woman who is strong, successful, and confident." Marissa stalked around the room now, engaging every woman in the room. "Don't *you* want to look like this? Don't you want people to notice you and see *at a glance* that you are bold, powerful, and secure within yourself?" The women in the room nodded; a few of them clapped and whooped. "This is what a courageous, fearless, and compelling woman looks like. This is what I can do for you. This, ladies, is the power of Beautiful Illuminations."

Every woman in the room had leapt to her feet, applauding and cheering.

Damn, this chick was good.

By the end of the night, she'd sold thousands of dollars' worth of makeup, vitamins, and other crap and signed up half of the attendees as consultants.

"You did great," Marissa said as she dropped me off at the Starbucks to pick up my car. "Oh, before I forget, here is your makeup kit, complete with application instructions. We want you to look your best when you meet Annabelle. Also, you should know that fifty percent of the party commissions go to you, my dear."

"What? I didn't even do anything."

"No, you did everything." That sinister smile curled her ridiculously pink lips. "It was because of you that every single woman there made a purchase. Their lives will change forever, thanks to BI, and that, honey, that was all you. See you at the big meeting on Friday!" she called as she drove away.

I wanted to throw up. No, I wanted to rid the world of the disease that was Beautiful Illuminations and all of its writhing hydra heads. I wanted to whip out my concealed Divinity blade, leap onto the hood of her Bentley, tear back the convertible top, and lop Marissa's head right off and then use it to lure Anabael out of hiding and do the same thing to her. But I couldn't. The head of one little consultant wasn't going to bring Anabael to the surface; if anything, it would only serve to send her scurrying back to the shadows, and Lord knew when we'd manage to pin her down again. Nope, I had to wait.

Shit, I hated waiting.

The next day, Lana and Isolde called me into the front room. The distinct smell of frankincense and betony wafted up from an incense pot surrounded by a ring of carnations, meadowsweet, and periwinkle in the middle of the end table. All of the furniture was pushed aside, leaving the end table in the center of the room. Isolde sat me down on the floor next to it and took my hands in hers.

"In the event that you're possessed, we need to ensure that you remain inside of your mind, even if it is just a glimmer of who you are. Spectorals effectively kill the core of a human when they enter, taking over mind, body, and soul. In essence, your human self simply ceases to exist. We cannot let that happen to you.

"Yet while you are human, as a hunter you are *more*. The gifts bestowed upon you by Gabriel make it so. With that in mind, Lana and I believe we can project a safe place inside your mind where you can keep free from her reach, a place for you to be able to fight her from within. To her, it will appear that she has control, and you *will* have to allow her to see parts of your mind you'd rather not. However, you can take some things into the safeness with you, just not much."

"Okay, then let's do this," I said. "What do I need to do? Do I need to choose now which thoughts I don't want her to see?"

"No, we are only going to perform the spell and create the space inside your mind. You will know when the time comes, and you will do wonderfully, as you always do." Isolde pushed my hair off of my face and behind my ear. She was the closest thing I had to a mother and more of a mother to me than the one I'd been born to. "Lie back and lay your head in my lap."

As I did, she gently settled her hands on either side of my head while Lana sat next to us and covered my heart, hand over hand. They stared at each other and started to speak. The words were quiet and I couldn't hear what they were saying, but I could see their lips moving in unison. My body felt oddly ethereal, and I closed my eyes, letting the weightlessness wash over me.

In the morning we enjoyed a real breakfast, the first one we'd had since leaving the mansion—not the prepackaged power bars or frozen toaster pastry things we'd been sustaining ourselves on lately. Man alive, I hadn't realized how much I missed Isolde's cooking.

I was loading the dishwasher when my phone rang on the other side of the counter. Furiously trying to dry my hands off, I picked up the phone to see it was Daniel.

"Hey," I said as I hopped onto the counter.

"There you are," Daniel said. "I was just getting ready to leave you a dirty voice mail."

"Well, then maybe I should hang up and let you call me back."

"You could, or I can just tell you now."

The smooth, sultry sound of his voice turned my body to Jell-O, and I could picture him…sitting in the middle of our bed, running his hand over his chest, that damned grin of his wide as can be as his tongue slid out from in between those gorgeous lips and curled over the top one. Jesus, I had to shake myself back into reality before I slid off the counter and into a puddle on the floor.

"You gotta stop that." I fanned myself, trying to calm down.

"Stop what?" The words rolled out of him so slowly and deliberately that I wanted to tear all my hair out. "I haven't even told you how much I miss the way your skin tastes, especially that spot at the top of your thigh. You know, right there in the crook? I haven't even begun to describe how badly I want to settle between those gorgeous legs of yours and li—"

"Daniel!" I shouted, my voice cracking, before I cupped my hand around the receiving end and whispered, "Let me get to my room."

Gripping the phone, I could hear his low chuckle as I raced up the stairs, praying I didn't run into anyone. Luckily, my path was clear, and I quickly shut the door behind me, making sure I locked that sucker. The last thing I needed was Tess—or worse, Isolde—walking in on me.

"Okay, I'm alone."

"Why did you want to be alone in your room when I tell you how much I want to lick between your legs?"

My breath caught and my knees started to wobble. I tried to answer him, I really did, but I couldn't seem to get my mouth to work.

"Is it so you could touch yourself, put your hand down the front of your pants, and stroke that sweet little spot, imagining that it's my tongue?"

"Yes," I said quietly.

"Good, then do it."

Flopping back on the bed, I quickly unbuttoned my jeans and kicked them off. With a shaky hand, I closed my eyes and ghosted down my belly and settled between my legs. The satin was damp, which shouldn't have surprised me.

"Don't cheat now," he said, low and raspy. "I want you underneath those panties, skin on skin, just like me."

My eyes popped open, and I could practically see him sprawled in the middle of our bed, naked as all get-out and gripping his hard length tightly as he smiled devilishly and licked his lips at me.

"Jesus," I panted as I shoved my hand under the elastic waistband of my panties. My fingers made contact with the soft, wet flesh and my hips bucked of their own accord.

"Oh, Evelyn," he moaned. "I can almost taste you on my bottom lip. I like to do that, save a little bit of you on my mouth so I can taste it when I'm inside of you."

My lower body pulsed against my hand as my fingers moved, circling and pressing, sliding in and out. I heard Daniel make that hot little growly noise he made just before he finished, and stars erupted behind my eyes as an orgasm rocketed through my body.

"I love you," he said, catching his breath. "Now go get that bitch."

Okay, I'd be the first person to admit it: that round of phone brown-chicken-brown-cow with Daniel was almost as good as the real thing.

Almost.

It was exactly what I needed, though; it eased just the right amount of stress and gave me just the right thing to remember before I headed into the belly of the beast, so to speak. Tonight was the big night, the Beautiful Illuminations regional sales meeting, and I had a golden ticket. Tonight I would be rubbing shoulders with some of the higher-up Specs, and if I was lucky, I'd get in there next to Anabael. If I was really lucky, I'd take her down. If I was really, *really* lucky, I wouldn't get my brain whammied.

To cover all our bases, Tony had us slap a GPS tracker on my car before I left for the meet and greet — he'd cleverly disguised it as the Chevrolet emblem. There was already one on my phone, but the way all of our tech had been acting up whenever I was around Marissa and her band of merry plastic minions, a backup was definitely in order. It was a good thing, too; this joint where the meeting was held was tucked back behind an abandoned warehouse — the one in Lana's vision, we could only presume — and surrounded by three layers of chain link fencing, complete with razor wire atop each one. This place was protected better than a prison, for shit's sake. They even had a guard shack that practically strip-searched me and my car before we were even allowed in the parking lot. Thank goodness I'd ditched my earpiece in my purse when I saw how locked down this place was.

Pulling into a parking space, I fished my earpiece out of my bag and shoved it in.

"You guys still there?" I pretended to fix my hair and ever so lovely clown makeup in the rearview mirror in case any security guards had eyes on me.

"Yeah, we're here," Tess said. "Are you in?"

"Not yet, but I think they got those guards from the Department of Corrections. They damn near had me bend over and cough."

"Sounds super fun. By the way, did I tell you that you look absolutely smashing in your Beautiful Illuminations uniform? I don't know if it's the gold lamé or the twelve layers of makeup, but I gotta be honest, with you, Ev, you made me a little wet."

"You're disgusting."

"Hey, just a heads-up, though. Right as you pulled out your earpiece, Lana went into another seizure. Isolde is with her trying to get a hold of her vi—but—so I'm going to—okay?"

"You're breaking up," I said just as someone knocked on my car window.

Of course it was one of Marissa's plastic posse waving me out of the car. What the hell was her name...Tawny, Tanya, Tiffany?

"Fuck," I muttered, jamming my lip-gloss into my purse.

"I'm so glad you made it," she said with a squeal, then pulled me into a tight bear hug that pushed the hard balls she had for boobs into my sternum. Ouch.

I reached up and tugged on my earlobe, trying to jiggle my earpiece. All I was getting though the damn thing was static, and that wasn't good.

"Yeah, I'm super excited," I said, trying to sound like I couldn't wait to get in there. The chick had her arm linked in mine and was pulling me toward the double glass doors at the front of the building. My cell phone ringing in my purse was the best sound I'd ever heard. Chatty Cathy didn't seem to hear it because she was still jawing like a monkey. I held up a finger in her face as I pulled out my phone and answered.

"Hey, girl, what's up?" I asked, moving ever closer to the building.

The voice on the other end of the line was patchy at best and sounded like she was thirteen thousand miles away and underwater. It vaguely sounded like Lana.

"Evelyn—don't—you do—understand?"

"What?" I yanked my arm free of what's-her-name's grip and pressed the phone tighter to my ear and cupped my hand over the other.

"Do no—the—whatev—do—stand?"

Before I could ask again, the phone was taken from me, and I wheeled around ready to deck that bitch when I realized we were standing directly in front of the glass doors and Marissa had my phone in her hand.

"No phones allowed, I'm afraid." She turned it off and handed it to a girl on her right. "We can't have anyone spilling our secrets to success, now can we?"

"Yeah, no, that's cool. I get it." I narrowed my eyes at her slightly. Something was different, but I couldn't put my finger on it. She looked exactly the same as she had a few nights ago; however, she sounded different. Not her voice, per se, but the way she spoke. The cadence of it had a strange cold edge, not the same used-up cheerleader pep as before.

Sweeping her hand in front of the door, the girl who had taken my phone opened the door and bowed slightly as we passed.

"Welcome to the inner sanctum of Beautiful Illuminations," Marissa said, hooking her arm in mine.

CHAPTER 14
DANIEL

Crammed in front of a giant monitor with Tony and Z, I watched Evie drive to this big BI meeting over the satellite feed. Alex hung back in the doorway, counting the links of the chain to his pocket watch. So far, so good. Tony had also patched us through to Ev's audio feed so we could hear the goings on. Things seemed to be running okay; we could hear her fine as she and Tess bantered back and forth. And then all hell broke loose.

A woman walked up to Evie's car, and while we could hear everything Tess said, Evie's voice was loaded with static, cutting in and out so badly that we couldn't even catch an entire word.

"Damn it," Tony mumbled as he wheeled across the room in his chair and fiddled with some kind of equipment.

Luckily, we still had a visual on her through the satellite feed. We saw her get out of the car and walk toward the warehouse with the woman who had approached her car. As they got closer to the building, Evie appeared to pull her phone out.

"Anthony, do we have audio on the phone?" Alex asked.

"Got it." And with a few clicks on Tony's keyboard, we could hear Lana's voice loud and clear.

"Evelyn, run. Don't go inside whatever you do. Do you understand?"

The hair on my arms raised. She wasn't running. It looked like she was trying to talk to Lana, but we couldn't hear a word.

"Do not go in there, whatever you do. Do you understand?"

Electricity raced up my backbone as I watched two women walk out of the warehouse. One of them plucked the phone right from Evie's hand and handed it to the other one.

I breathed faster, waiting for Ev to do something. Any second now, she was going to open up her can of whoop-ass and go off on these women. Or she was going to haul ass back to her car and drive out of there like a bat out of hell. Something, anything other than what she did do — she walked right into the building.

I stared at the screen, and the warehouse seemed to stare back, laughing at me through the soft whir of static that filled the room.

Emotion overtook me, and the hard linoleum of the floor connected with my knees as I crumpled. I couldn't control my breathing; the air rushed in and out faster and faster with every inhale and exhale. My body curled around itself, my arms coming up over my head. She was in there alone. Alone and blind and not knowing what was in store for her.

"Daniel, buddy, you gotta calm down," I heard, the words coming at me as if I was in a tunnel. The next thing I knew, giant arms were uncurling me and shoving a paper bag up to my mouth. "That's it, brother, breathe. Easy, you knew this was going to happen."

When I opened my eyes, I saw Z crouched down in front of me, holding the paper bag.

"Thanks," I said into it, and I took over holding it.

"S'okay, man." He plopped into the chair next to mine. We both looked blankly at the image on the monitor in front of us, the live satellite feed of the warehouse Evie had just disappeared into.

"I hate that she's in there by herself," I said quietly.

"Me, too." Z crossed his arms over his broad chest. "The thing is, I know damn well as sure as you do that if there is anyone in this house that can handle themselves in there alone, it's her."

"Yeah," I said on a sigh, refusing to take my eyes off of the monitor.

"Doesn't make you feel any better, though, does it?" he asked.

"Not even a little bit."

"I also know that you are the only reason she will make it out of this. The woman has a stubborn streak like you wouldn't believe.

Once she sets her mind to something…" He shook his head with a chuckle. "Let's just say I pity the idiot who tries to get in her way."

"Ain't that the truth."

"I knew a long time ago that if anyone was lucky enough to get past all her thick-headedness and down to her heart, she'd latch on to them and never let go. Part of me hoped that I could be that person, but something in her eyes, the way she looked through me and not at me, told me that I just wasn't. She looks *into* you, not through you. And I knew you felt the same for her the second I saw the way you look at her. Not everyone gets to have what you two have." Z turned to me and eyeballed the tattoo covering my head. "It's good to see you appreciate it."

"I do." I nodded. I knew Ev and Z had been fuck buddies, once—and only once—upon a time, and I accepted that as past. I was glad to hear that he did as well. "I'd do anything for her. She's my life, period."

Over the next hour, we had all paced the room at some point, waiting for something to happen, for some sign from Evie. Nothing. There wasn't even a breeze to rattle the leaves of the trees that we could see in the feed. Stone silence was the worst kind of silence.

"Are you sure the image hasn't frozen?" I asked, again.

Tony rubbed his temples. "For the gazillionth time, yes, I'm sure the image is live."

I opened my mouth to apologize but sucked in a breath as pain lanced across my chest, burning just under my left peck. Tony made the same sound, and I looked over to see him raising his shirt. The tattoo we'd all been marked with, the one that bound us all to one another as a hunting team, was glowing bright red.

"It's happening," I said, not realizing I'd spoken the words out loud until Tony answered.

"What's happening?"

"It! The thing, the—agh!" Agony burrowed through the center of my body and began to climb up my spine. The back of my head felt as if someone had just lit my hair on fire. Then I remembered I didn't have any hair left, and I turned to see my reflection in one of

Tony's monitors. The glow of the purple ink crawled across my scalp as if it had a life of its own, igniting every marking of Evie's name.

I heard the distinct sound of someone running up the hall and saw Alex skid into the room, his chest heaving from exertion. "They—" His words died when his eyes met mine.

He didn't have to say it. I knew it. I don't know how I knew it, but I knew it with every single cell in my body.

CHAPTER 15
EVELYN

I was marched into the lobby. It was impressive; I'll give it that much. There was an upside-down trapezoidal desk that swept up on one side, creating a separation between the receptionist and a small canopied seating area. The words *Beautiful Illuminations* were written across the back wall in giant three-dimensional letters, and another one of those Barbie clones sat perched behind the front desk. She smiled at me as she answered the phone and, like the other girl, bowed toward Marissa. My hunter instincts began screaming, and I planted my feet, pulling Marissa to a stop.

"Hey, you know what? I get the whole no-phone thing, I do, but I really have to call my friend back before we get started—"

"No," Marissa said sternly, yanking me toward the door to the right of the desk, before she schooled her attitude and pasted her happy face back on. "What I mean is, there's no point, really. You couldn't use a phone here even if you wanted to."

"Excuse me?" I dug in my heels.

"The building is fixed with voltage-controlled oscillators. They generate radio signals that interfere with a cell signal. Like I said, we have to protect our assets. This way, even if some unsavory individual manages to smuggle some kind of electronic device, like an earpiece, digital recorder, or something of that nature, it would be rendered useless."

Quickly, I went over the layout of the lobby. If I could break the hold she had on me, I could run, use the side of that desk as a launching pad, and bolt for the door and try to make it to my car. I would have to drive through three chain link fences to get the hell out of there, but I had to try.

My body tensed, ready for action when Marissa's grip tightened on my arm for a second before she relaxed her hold and slipped my hand through the crook of her arm. The other lady, the one from the parking lot, grabbed my free arm and did the same before I could jump into escape mode, and the two of them all but propelled me through the door next to the desk. Damn but they were surprisingly strong.

Once they got me inside, I saw a room filled with women, all politely seated in front of a big stage.

"Welcome everyone!" Marissa called as we started up the path down the center of the place, pulling me along between her and the other woman. They were both so tall, Amazonian really, and I had to practically run to keep up with them.

The room erupted with cheers as the three of us took to the stage. A giant spotlight popped on, and I squinted at the ultra-bright light.

"We have someone very special with us tonight," Marissa began, and the women in the room cheered. I could hear the folding chairs they'd been sitting on scraping and clattering to the floor.

Finally, I was going to lay eyes on my target—Anabael. Well, in her current form, anyway. I tried to will my eyesight to adjust to the blinding light so I could see where she was coming from.

"Who among us has not wished for this day? I tell you, none. Every one of you have been chosen to be here based on the amazing work you have done with Beautiful Illuminations, and as your reward, you shall bear witness. You can all rejoice in the knowledge that you were a part of taking Beautiful Illuminations to the next level."

My head whipped around, and I stared up at Marissa only to find her smiling down at me as she took my hand in hers and raised it over my head as if in triumph.

"Behold, the woman that we have been longing for, the hope beyond hope, the warrior in the weeds, the legendary hunter here in the glorious flesh...Evelyn Brighton!"

What the holy hell? I was smack-dab in the middle of a fucking ambush!

I wrenched myself free and leapt from the stage, whipping off my jacket in midair as I released the spell that kept my Divinity blade hidden. Reaching over my shoulder, I gripped the hilt and ripped it free of the scabbard, settling into a fighting stance.

But before I could activate the weapon, I happened to see the look on Marissa's face. Pure excitement and anticipation washed over her. She'd been waiting for this moment. She wanted me to activate the blade, which is precisely why I resisted the urge to do so.

With an eerie calm, she descended the steps from the stage and circled around me, looking me over from head to toe like I was some prized heifer. In response, all of the tattoos on my exposed skin glowed with power, casting light on the faces of all the women that had huddled around us. Lowering my weapon, I took a second look at the room. It was massive, about the size of one of those hotel ballrooms, and there was a good hundred and fifty women in there, easy. Their folding chairs had been discarded and shoved aside in a pile.

I expected to see some of them make a move, to speak up and ask what was going on or leap to Marissa's aid or something. But not a single one of them stirred. They all just stood in the middle of the room, gathered around us like a horde of zombies, waiting for instruction.

Looking back to Marissa, I saw—over in the corner, tucked behind the stage—a body crumpled on the floor. A blond.

Marissa followed my line of sight and sauntered over to the unconscious woman. As she flipped her over with the toe of her stiletto, I saw that the blond was the woman who claimed to be Annabelle Simmons, the head of Beautiful Illuminations. And she wasn't just unconscious, she was freaking dead.

"This body served me well," Marissa said, squatting down and stroking the blond hair, "but humans age so quickly, don't they? Their skin sagging off their bones and taking on the texture of crêpe paper before you know it."

She stood and smoothed the fine silk suit she wore. "Now *this* body has done well in a pinch. A nice little transition piece, if you will. Just took it on earlier today because I wanted to be in something familiar to you so I could see your face when you realized what was going to happen. Well, that and I couldn't bear to be in that other one for another second. However, I can almost feel gravity pulling on this flesh, dragging it down with its invisible hands. But you, a hunter, your body will not age. I could become a true Goddess within you."

"Not if I have anything to say about it." I couldn't risk the possibility that Isolde and Lana's safe room in my mind wouldn't work. There was only one thing I could do—I had to end this here and now. I flipped my sword end over end in my hands and raised it over my head. Spectorals needed a living host, and if this was the only way to keep that crunty bitch out of my head, that's how it would have to be. "I'm sorry, Daniel," I whispered as I prepared to slash the weapon down into my own chest.

Nothing happened. My arms didn't move, not a single inch. The room full of women had moved as one, grappling my wrists, arms, shoulders, hips, waist, every inch of my body, virtually freezing me in place. One of them pulled away from the group and stood before me. As she reached for my sword, she was blasted back from the power the weapon emanated. Anabael waded through the throng and slowly unbuckled the scabbard strapped to my back. Raising the leather casing over my head, she slipped it over the blade and took the shielded weapon.

"I will enjoy playing with this very soon," she crooned, stroking the leather-covered steel.

"Have fun trying." I laughed. "You saw what it did to Betty the Barbie over there. My blade only works for me."

Anabael handed the scabbard off to one of the women and stood directly in front of me. Reaching out, she stroked the backs of her manicured fingers down my cheek.

"Darling girl, you don't seem to get it. Before the night is over, I will *be* you."

"I will be you."

Those four words banged around inside my skull, trying like hell to wheedle their way into the part of my mind that held on to the possibility I would still be me when I left.

The sea of women began to move, and I could feel my body moving with them.

Okay, Evs, get your head on right. Deep down, on some level, you knew this was going to happen. This was the reason you got bonded to Daniel. You are strong in body and mind, and that was why you were chosen. Now suck your shit up right now.

The tide pulled me through the big room and toward a bank of doors in the back, behind the stage. One by one, the doors popped open, and the wave of women spilled through the openings, carrying me with them. Flanked on all sides, I was taken into the next room that appeared to have no walls, ceiling, or floor. Every inch of the room was painted black to give a feeling of sensory deprivation. I knew there was a floor; I could feel the concrete under my shoes, but at the same time I had the bizarre feeling that I was floating.

When the movement stopped, I found myself standing in front of the biggest pillar candle I'd ever seen in my life. The damn thing came up to my chest, just under my chin—a good four feet of blood-red wax with three wicks as thick as my thigh. Anabael stood on the other side, a maniacal grin splitting her face.

I'd been face to face with some of the most vicious and evil creatures on this world and the next. Heck, I'd even stared into the eyes of Lucifer himself. But I'd never had a deeper, more intense feeling of dread in my life.

I. Am. Screwed.

One hundred percent, Grade A, USDA screwed.

The memory of last night came barreling at me—the spell Isolde and Lana had worked on me—and as I stood in the black room in front of that big-ass candle, I had to do two things.

One, I had to resolve myself to the fact that this *was* going to happen. Daniel wasn't going to burst through the door in the nick of time. Anabael's Spectoral self was going to leave Marissa's body and jump into mine, and there wasn't anything I could do to stop it. Period.

Two, I had to reach into myself and lock away everything I held sacred. She was going to know Daniel was a hot button for me the second she got into my head; that couldn't be helped, but I could close up the details of our love. I *had* to lock that up. At least I had to try.

I closed my eyes and started to concentrate. When nothing appeared to happen as I perused the inside of my own head, I started to wonder…had the incantation worked? They didn't on the rare occasion, and the way things were going with this assignment, it wouldn't

have surprised me in the slightest if Anabael had some sort of coun-
teractive black magic that knocked all of my own magic impotent.

I was about ready to give up the ghost when I saw something
flicker. An imagined door opened; this had to be the backdoor to my
mind. As fast as I could, I shoved it all in there—the small touches
when we were alone, the soft words whispered in the middle of the
night, the pieces of my heart that were only for him. I crammed all
of it into the back of my brain, pushing the thoughts deep into the
dark corners and burying them under the surface stuff—the sparring, the heat, and the mind-numbing sex. Not that I wanted her to
have access to any part of Daniel, but he was too prominent in my
mind to hide it all. Like Isolde had said, I had to allow Anabael to
see *something* if I wanted to keep anything secure.

I backed into the safe house tucked into my cerebral cortex and
closed the door tight. If this bitch wanted anything in here, she was
going to have to fight me so hard for it there wouldn't be any of my
gray matter left that would be useful.

When I opened my eyes again, Anabael was still there, that warped
smile wide. On closer inspection, I could see dark circles form and
crow's feet spider out from the corners of her eyes and mouth, the
edges of her lips puckering and crinkling.

"You're not looking so hot there," I said, nodding to the acceler-
ated aging going on before my very eyes. I had always heard that
one of the telltale signs of a Spectoral getting ready to leave the host
was lightning-speed aging; the being inside sucked up every ounce
of nutrients that it could, breaking down cells as it went.

She raised one bony hand and inspected it, turning it this way
and that. The skin slid like wet tissue paper over the bulging veins and
knuckles.

"Yes, this body is so very synthetic, much older than it appears to
be." She looked at me, her eyes sinking deeper and deeper into the
sockets. She walked around the candle and stood next to me. Pushing my hair over my ear, she trailed her finger through the strands.

"So lovely." She gripped my chin and tilted my head to the side.
"The things I will do with this body. You look so innocent and trust-
worthy, I'd imagine people would kill each other just to stand in the
same room with such purity."

"I wouldn't fucking bet on it," I snarled.

Anabael threw her Marissa head back and laughed so loudly it echoed off the black walls.

"Such spirit. That will remain in your bones once I take over your mind and body, and it will only serve to further your appeal to humans."

Sidling up close, she placed one skeletal arm around my shoulders to pull me near. With her free hand, she pointed to the center of the giant pillar of wax.

"Do you see there, the three wicks?" She spoke so softly and close to my ear, as if she was a mother figure sharing the great secrets of life with me, and it made the surface of my skin ripple with revulsion. "They look like simple, ordinary lengths of cotton, don't they? I can assure you they are anything but. Those three fibers hold within them the power to change the world. One represents the horrid train wreck of a body that I currently reside in. That shall be lit first. The one in the center represents my Spectoral self, my true self. Once that one is lit, my spirit will be pulled from this flesh and remain suspended until the final wick is lit. That one is you. This final lighting will draw you out of that glorious, unaging hunter body and open up the way for me to occupy your essence. It's quite a lovely process, don't you think?"

"If by 'lovely' you mean extremely creepy and messed up nine ways from Sunday, then, yeah, it's really fuckin' lovely."

Coiling up all of my strength, I burst backward with my head, clocking whoever was behind me right in the nose so hard I could feel the blood in my hair. The hands on my shoulders loosened and I tried to wriggle free, but I was trapped between Anabael and her minions. Before I could ball up a fist to start punching my way out, I was grabbed again and held into place. Anabael surged forward against me, her acrylic nails biting into the back of my scalp as she cranked my head back.

"Don't ruin this day for me," she growled into my ear. "Do you know how long I've been waiting for this? How many years I've bided my time for just the right body? Centuries, so many centuries that I'd all but given up on getting inside one of you. A hunter, one glorious hunter that I could crawl inside of, and then I heard of you, the great Evelyn Brighton, the veritable star of the unflappable Lebriga Corporation, and now I have you all to myself." Her nose skimmed up the side of my neck. "Did you know that the human body smells different from the inside? As wonderful as it smells on the outside, it's so much better from the inside, especially when you weren't born of flesh. When I came into existence, there was no birth, no miracle of life. I simply wasn't and then I was, swirling around, trying to find shape in the brimstone mists of Hell."

She released my head and began strolling back and forth on the other side of the candle. Her stare held mine, boring so hard that I could practically see Anabael staring out through Marissa's eyes.

"For nearly a millennia I served, doing as I was told like a good little Spectoral minion. But then I got tired of being a cog in the mechanism. I wanted to be more than part of the engine, I wanted—no, I *needed* to be the operator of it all. So I played the game. I sidled up to Lucifer and learned everything I could, and when everyone was busy at their menial tasks of death and destruction, I escaped the confines of Hell. I unleashed myself into your world to fulfill my destiny."

"Destiny?" I laughed. "You don't have a body, but you have a freaking destiny? You know, I've heard some ridiculous shit from some ridiculous demons, but that has *got* to take the cake."

"I have a body!" she shouted, leaning over the candle. She got directly into my face for a moment before appearing to gather her control and settle back into her place on the other side of the pillar. "Your body."

The hands holding me in place gripped me tight, lengthening my legs and snapping my arms out taut. The sound of a match striking echoed off of every surface and ricocheted around the inside of my head.

Shitballs. This was it. I tried to move, to do anything I could to get free, but I was all but frozen in midair, held a good foot off the ground by more hands than I could count.

A taper candle came around my head, into my periphery, and ended up in Anabael's hand.

Fuck. Everything started to shake. Every muscle trembled with a mixture of fear and anxiety.

The whites of Anabael's eyes shrank away, eaten up by a black cloud that filled up her sockets.

"Say goodnight, Gracie," she said with a grin as she touched the fire to the first wick.

Wind whipped around the room—from where, I hadn't a clue because there wasn't a window in the joint. The flame licked and wavered, leaning toward Anabael. Marissa's body slithered to the ground as if what had held her upright had leached out of her. As she hit the floor, the middle wick ignited and fizzled just as fast, sending up a plume of smoke. The third wick caught, and I froze.

I didn't feel any differently. I looked around and noticed everyone's focus was still trained on the center of the candle. What the hell? Had something gone wrong?

Then I saw it—the smoke from the center wick, twirling and gliding through the air as if it had life. Staring at the morphing gray cloud, I felt the presence of Anabael. It was her, or the essence of her, trapped in the smoke. The puff of vapor danced closer, billowing out toward my face. On pure instinct, I shut my mouth and stopped my breathing. The cloud seemed to jiggle, as if in laughter, as it moved around my head. I snapped my eyes shut. I could feel the smoke ghosting over my face in some twisted caress. The sensation pushed over the shells of my ears and into the canals.

My head swam. I wasn't sure if it was from Anabael's invasion or the fact that I seriously needed to breathe. If I could only…only what? I would have to breathe at some point, and by the weird feeling in my ears, she was going to get in whether I took a breath or not.

The gasp ripped out of me, sucking much-needed oxygen into my lungs. Unfortunately, that wasn't all that came in.

I could feel her, moving under my skin, sliding her way along my bone, skipping through my veins. The sensation crawled up my neck, a sour taste filling my mouth, and then…yes, the scent of brimstone exploding inside my nose.

Gritting my teeth, I pushed back with my mind. The tattoo on my sixth rib burned, and I could feel the power inside of me grow, strengthening my will to fight for my mind.

Cackling echoed in my ears, a sound so sinister it made my blood run cold.

"How sweet. Your fellow hunters are trying to help you." The voice in my head wasn't mine or what I'd heard coming from the mouth of Marissa; it was wicked and shrill, like the sound of nails on a chalkboard. "I can feel them all against me, trying to push me out."

The malevolent laughter began again, banging around inside my head, making it feel like my eyeballs were going to pop out and shoot across the room.

My body snapped of its own accord, jerked and flailed as if there were strings attached to everything and Anabael was working me like a meat puppet. The cramped feeling inside my body grew, crowding me out of my own brain until my consciousness pressed against the base of my skull. I could practically see her red eyes staring at me, shrinking me into absolute and total oblivion.

I felt my body go limp. My eyes drifted closed, and everything went dark.

CHAPTER 16
ANABAEL

Moving from one body to another could be quite the pleasant and exhilarating experience, when the host was a willing participant. Conversely, when transitioning into an unwilling host, I found that it would leave the physical body drained and unable to function very well for a few days after the transition.

But this creature, this hunter, was not like the others. Make no mistake, she fought me—oh yes, she fought hard. She clawed and scratched and pushed against the inevitable, and yet I wasn't hampered by your average human reluctance. Surely it somehow had to do with the fact that she was not the average human. In addition, I could feel the power inside of her instantaneously. I stretched out under her skin, taking in the raw strength coiled in her muscles, just waiting to be utilized. Knowledge began to unfold, everything I could ever want to know about the society of hunters and their non-hunting partners.

Yes, this was what I had wanted the most, the wisdom behind that wretched sect of demon killers—their strengths, weaknesses, and every slice of information in between. Where to strike first to infiltrate and consume, turning the members of this Lebriga Corporation against themselves until I owned every single hunter. I'd been so patient, waiting for this moment to arrive. From the second I'd learned what a hunter could do, the potential that lingered deep in their old bones, I had longed to possess one. Finally, now that I was inside of one—the most powerful one—I would have an army, the one I needed, the one I *deserved*. The one that would raise me up as their Goddess.

My new chest expanded as I took my first deep breath. Ahhh, this was decadence in its finest hour. I was on the right path. I could feel it in the very cells of this body.

Flipping my lids open, I stared out at my followers with fresh eyes. The vision was impeccable, flawless. I'd never been behind eyes this magnificent; it was as if the world was my very own high-definition television. I looked down at my arms and saw the markings, each individual stretch of ink, even the ones that couldn't be seen by the human eye. Words, spells pushed forward to the front of my brain, and I spoke one. A patch of ink illuminated around my wrist, and I felt added strength surge into that hand. Turning to the closest human, I balled up my fist, cranked back, and landed a punch so hard I felt the woman's jawbone shatter beneath my knuckles. I waited for the pain to take over my hand, but it was so minimal it might as well have not even bothered to show up.

I looked down at the woman, writhing on the floor in pain, and I couldn't help but wonder how strong I actually was in this body. Kneeling down next to her, I took her face in my hands. Her eyes filled with confusion over what had happened, yet they pleaded for the pain to end. I had to know what I was capable of, and there was only one way to find out. That information was…What did they call it?…"mission critical."

"The needs of the many, my child," I murmured before I gripped her head and twisted it as hard as I could. I heard the crack of her neck, felt the snap of the bone ricochet up my arm. I'd never felt this powerful in all the bodies I'd inhabited over the years combined.

Dropping her lifeless body to the ground, I shoved it aside with my foot. Standing to my full height, I reared back and roared like a mighty lioness.

I peered out over the sea of women, each of them a Spectoral cloaked in human flesh. I was now not only their leader by matter of age and wisdom, but sheer, raw strength. That little display denoted that fact, and they all knew it. One by one, they bowed to me as I passed, kissing my hand when they could and pressing it to their foreheads in honor. The physical and psychological power swelled within me.

"This is just the beginning, my daughters," I announced. "I shall lead you all into the light. You shall be at my side when I crush this society of hunters and bring them into *my* society of followers." The grunts and purrs of approval echoed in the black room.

When I signaled her, a follower tucked into the corner of the room smiled and walked to open the door along the back wall. Ten naked human males filed out in a single line, shackled wrist to ankle and chained to one another. Each one had been chosen carefully for his physical beauty, the length and girth of his manhood, and his ability to breed, of course.

"We shall milk these males and others like them of their seed so that we may grow our sisterhood." I perused each specimen, running my fingers along their taut muscles and sculpted cheekbones. The last one, the tallest, most virile male, sucked his full bottom lip into his mouth and groaned in pleasure as I cupped and stroked his length.

His low whisper of "Please, mistress, use me," made the growing want inside me *to* use him shrivel, the wetness in my center drying up as he pushed his all too willing cock against my hand.

"We shall keep a choice few for our carnal pleasures and feast on the ones that remain. We shall take their flesh into our own, and I declare that their knowledge and strength shall be absorbed within us. As I say it, it shall be so."

That last bit was directed to the three women against the back wall who were feverishly scribbling on pads of paper. My scribes, the three had been at my side when I'd broken free from Hell, noting every step I'd taken on this journey through the centuries—every movement and utterance to this very moment when all I'd worked for began to coalesce. They would write what would be the new Bible.

My Bible.

This world and the planes of existence surrounding it would no longer pray and cower to a male deity, good or evil. They would bow and pay homage to the new Goddess of both worlds.

Me.

I would revel in the sight of the mighty Lucifer falling to his knees before me, begging for my forgiveness and mercy like so many had done before him, myself included. He would rue the day he'd ever set me aside for a new plaything or forced me to inhabit the body of some revolting man. He would see what I could do when

I wielded the power of Gabriel's pack of dutiful hunters. The scope of the new world would revolve around the greater sex, the raw feminine omnipotence that had been repressed for far too many lifetimes. Women's liberation would take on a whole new meaning, and I would be at the forefront, defining the parameters. I would no longer take direction from any man, of any species or supernatural plane, and this body would thank me for it.

"Gather, my daughters," I called, "as I prepare to go forth into the first of many hunter dens. I wish for you to enjoy the pleasures I have chosen for you. Use them all and use them well. To destiny!"

"Destiny!" they all echoed, raising their hands in the air in a reverent salute.

Scraps of clothing began to fly around the room as the women took to their prizes—two and three women at a time, grinding and writhing against each slave. The men' chains rattled as the woman took them. Oh, how I loved the sound the metal links made when they clanged together. I strode over to the eager one and squatted down next to him. Picking up one of his large hands, I took his middle finger into my mouth and then slid the thick, moistened digit under my skirt. His finger pushed in and out of me as I leaned over to speak to the woman riding him like a glorious she-beast.

"When everyone is well spent and their desires fully and properly satiated, feed on this one."

His eyes widened in horror as I pulled his finger from my body and bent it back until it snapped. He began to plead, not to give pleasure but for his life. How I wanted to raise up my skirt and silence him, fill his pathetic mouth with my pussy, to feel his cries for his last breath vibrate against my clit until I came. But I hadn't the time, and the fear now raised in him would make his meat all the sweeter for my daughters to consume.

I rose and straightened my clothing, smoothing out the crumpled skirt and patting down my hair as the next part of my plans renewed my desire.

In the skin of this hunter, I would infiltrate their home, and I would do so flawlessly. They knew there was a possibility I would possess her, but that's all they knew it to be—a possibility.

One small kink in masking myself as Evelyn was the fact that I wouldn't be able to use her phone or earpiece without an unusual amount of unexplained static. Being inside of her head, I knew that she had figured out that my kind didn't mix well with electronics. I was going to have to devise a plausible reason, and there was only one that made sense.

I selected four of the largest women. They would need to attack me and beat this hunter's body nearly to a pulp because it had to appear as though she'd narrowly escaped with her life. It was the only way to make it believable.

Walking toward the lobby with the chosen four, out of the corner of my eye I saw the hunter's sword on the black lacquer table against the back wall. Wrapped in a leather casing so fine and buttery soft, it almost seemed delicate.

"Wait," I announced. With the weapon in my sights, I veered off my previous course to the lobby, strode over, and took the scabbard in my hand. This was a mighty blade, that much I knew; what I wasn't sure of was if I'd be able to wield it. In theory, I was in the hunter's body, so I *was* her in essence; therefore, I should be able to take the sword in my hand.

With a deep breath, I raised my hand over the hilt and gripped the end.

White-hot pain shot up my arm, and energy coursed through my body, rattling my teeth and all but forcing my hand to release. Cursing, I saw smoke curl from my palm; the pattern around the weapon's handle had burned into my flesh, glowing red as if in warning. It was a good thing that I ran into this issue here with my followers. This could have posed a big problem had it happened in front of the other hunters.

Blowing the smoke off my palm, I motioned for the four women to follow me. We stepped into the lobby, and as per my instruction, they pummeled Evelyn's body, punching and kicking until I spat red.

I struggled up off of the floor, wiped the blood from my mouth, and gathered Evelyn's belongings. Pouring myself into her car, I searched her mind for the way back to their lair. The location that came to the front of her memory was a modest home nearby, a stakeout location that she'd been staying at.

"Shit," I sputtered, my shaking hands fumbling with the key in the ignition. The vehicle sprang to life, and the digital clock on the dashboard showed that it was just after midnight. I let the memory portion of Evelyn's brain take over and lead me to the house where her cohorts were holed up. As much as I wanted to get into the main house where all the hunters were, I would have to continue to exercise a modicum of patience. Convince the three, no, *four* women at the stakeout home that I was Evelyn and that my cover had been blown. That the crew would need to regroup at the main house and form another plan of attack. Yes, that was what had to happen.

By the time I pulled the car into the garage, I could barely see out of the one eye that hadn't swollen shut. Every breath I took screamed with pain, which wasn't surprising as I was certain this body had sustained at least a couple of broken ribs during the beating.

Before the garage door could roll down behind the vehicle, a small woman flew through the door leading into the house, screeching at the top of her lungs. I recognized her from Evelyn's memories as Tess, her handler.

"What the holy fuck? The guys lost contact with you over five hours ago. I mean, they saw you stumble out of the lobby and get into the car, but what happened in—" She stopped mid-sentence as I struggled to stand. "Jesus, Evs, you actually fought her off, didn't you? I mean, damn, girl, I knew you were good, but even I'm impressed with that shiz. You look like hell, though. You should've called for backup, or at the very least for a pickup."

"They took my phone," I mumbled, finding that the inside of my mouth was swollen and speech was difficult.

She put her hands on her petite hips and glared for a moment before she shook her head. "And naturally you're too much of a pig-headed asshole to call for help anyway. Let's get you inside and get you cleaned up."

Helping me out of the car and into the house, Tess placed me on a couch in the living room while she ran off to get someone named Isolde. While I waited, I heard footsteps in the hallway. As a tall blond woman rounded the corner, she jerked to a stop. Lana, her name was Lana. She looked at Evelyn strangely, as if she wasn't certain about…something. Reaching back into Evelyn's thoughts to access her personality, I spoke.

"Christ, do I look that bad?"

She blinked at me, once, twice, and by the third time, her hands went to her temples, massaging them.

"No," she said with an accent. "Well, yes, you do look very bad, but my head, it is not…how you say, on right. I can't see anything through the pain."

I struggled to hold back the smile while I thought on how Evelyn might respond to that.

"That sucks. Wanna trade?" I mentally crossed my fingers that I'd gotten what she would say right.

Lana smiled and chuckled. Yes, I'd gotten it right.

By that time, Tess and two other women came into the room. My eyes widened as much as they could through the swelling. One was Maria, Lana's handler, coming in to take her back to her room to lie down. And the other, Isolde, I knew. I knew her not from Evelyn's memory banks but my own. The name alone hadn't rung any bells, but I had never forgotten the face of someone who had tried to kill me—even if the last time I'd seen it had been over a thousand years ago.

My time in England was done. Lucifer would allow me and the band of six Spectorals I'd been working with to leave these bodies for new ones. Bodies that would be stronger and heartier, people across the sea to the north—Vikings. The move would be simple once we'd returned to our non-corporeal forms. We'd simply move over the ocean like a mist and possess the first humans we made contact with. I would be the last to disengage from my host as I was the only one strong enough to separate on my own.

The rocks smacked together as I piled one on top of the other, covering the six empty bodies. Half of my team was already making their way to the north, while the other half stayed behind to keep watch while I cleaned up the discarded carcasses. The air around me thickened, a clear sign that one of my cohorts had entered the cave where we were leaving the bodies.

"Humans approach," a ghostly voice hissed in the vicinity of my ear. "Three, possibly four. You must make haste and leave that body behind. They bear the stench of hunters."

"No, they will not run me out of my rightful vessel before I'm prepared to leave it. Let them come, and, Maron, fetch Sesek and Edaral. We must make an example of hunters that dare to think they can thwart Lucifer's plans."

Maron, Sesek, and Edaral floated around me as I stood, bold as you please, in the center of the cave. I would not cower in the corner or lie in wait behind a rock. No, they would see what the Fates had in store for them.

The three hunters entered the seaside cave, and I swept the skirts of my gown out to either side of me. I gave them a slight nod of my head. That's all they would get from me; I would not bow in greeting as was customary. The body I inhabited was a young, pretty girl that looked to be an angel delicately placed on this earth to frolic among the humans. I smiled and spread my arms in invitation.

"Welcome," I said in my sweetest voice, "to Hell."

Edaral lead the Spectoral attack, screaming like the wraith that he was and sliding into the gaped open mouth of one of the hunters, knocking him to the ground.

Maron covered the flesh of one of the other hunters and the woman cried in pain, dropping her sword and falling to the sand pleading to be let free.

And Sesek, ah, but she was my favorite. She slid up the final hunter, caressing him, whispering in his ear the most erotic scenarios that she could imagine — she could get a priest to throw his robes up in the middle of a town square and move as if he were fucking the thin air. But that was just where she began. Before he could finish his lustful actions, she gained just enough control of his body to make him castrate himself. This time, however, she entered the hunter's body like a ripple, making his flesh bubble in her wake as she seated herself inside of him.

I watched as the three hunters writhed in pain, clawing at their scalps in a feeble effort to free their brains. I had been so wrapped up in the enjoyment of the hunters' torment, I did not hear the fourth enter. The great whooshing sound of her sword zinged past my ear, the pain tight as the very edge of the blade touched the shell.

Spinning around, I saw her, the vile creature with her sword.

"That was but in warning. I want you to see the one who is going to relieve you of your head. B'taek ch'llo!*" she spat at me as she raised her weapon over her head and made for another pass.*

"Theurgistic whore—" I laughed "—you will not best me with your silly spells and charms. Be gone before I consume you as I have your fellow hunters."

As the words left my mouth, I could feel a pull on my Spectoral center. Raising a hand to my ear, I felt the wound, its blood burning my fingers, and I looked up to see the witch grinning at me.

"My blade has been treated, you arrogant demon. Not only will you go back to Hell, but you will stay down there. B'taek, b'taek ch'llo!"

With a deep breath, I shed my human form like a cloak, watching as the shell slithered to the ground at her feet.

"We are not finished, Anabael. Run now, but mark my words, you and I are far from finished."

Oh, but taking down this band of hunters just got better.

"What happened?" Isolde asked as she knelt beside me.

"I was made, and then they all jumped me. I tried to get to my blade, but there were too many of them. I barely made it out of there as it was."

"Well, don't worry, we'll…" She picked up one of my hands and started to inspect the damage. "Odd." She picked up the other hand and examined the knuckles and fingernails. "Your defensive wounds are usually the worst, but I don't see any."

Fuck.

"I told you, there were too many."

"Mm, yes, you did say that." She laid my hand back down and began to prod around my eyes and mouth, mopping up dried blood with a wet cloth. "Where else do you hurt?"

"I think I have some broken ribs—shit that fucking hurts! Try to be more careful," I hissed.

Her eyes snapped to mine and her head tilted slightly. "Indeed, my apologies."

Looking over her shoulder, I saw Tess standing in the doorway with an open jar of ointment. She was frozen where she stood, one eyebrow cocked over her widened eyes.

"Dude, did you just snap at Iz?" she asked. "You better watch it, girl. She's the one with all the healing mojo. Plus, that's like yelling at your mom. You just don't do that shit."

"It's all right." Isolde gave a small smile, the look in her eyes warm and caring. "I'm a big girl. I can handle myself."

"Regardless, it's my job to knock her ass down a peg or two when it's needed," Tess said. "And I don't care if she did just get her clock cleaned. She needs to respect you. Period."

"She's right," I said. I had to maintain this façade until we got into the main house. "I'm sorry, Izzy, it won't happen again."

"Damn right it won't happen again," Tess muttered. "By the way, assuming your cover is blown, I called the guys at the house. Alex wants us back ASAP. No sense in us hanging out here any longer than we have to."

"Yeah." I nodded. "These Spectorals are smarter than you think. We need to come up with another way to get to them."

"Indeed." Isolde slathered a healthy dollop of ointment onto my face. "They are quite clever, but we're smarter." She looked at me, and for a split second I was certain she knew I was not Evelyn; however, it was so fast I wasn't sure if it had actually happened. I would have to watch myself around this one.

I couldn't think about that now. We were going back to their lair, and by this time next week, I would have the entire team under my reign.

CHAPTER 17
EVELYN

Light began to return, dim, but definitely light. I tried to stretch, but I couldn't move. I tried to focus my vision, but my eyes wouldn't cooperate either. They no longer seemed like my own but two underwater television screens that had really horrid reception, portholes to a world that I was no longer a part of. Sound was muted, mumbled like the adults in a Charlie Brown cartoon. Every touch felt as if it was through layers, a mere ghost of a sensation. Then suddenly I felt my body move. My mouth was speaking, but they weren't my words.

Fucking hell, I was trapped inside my own skin, trapped behind Anabael.

I wasn't sure how much time had passed — hours, days, weeks even — or how much I had left before Anabael had my body for good. Time had become irrelevant, the very concept of it lost in this space inside my head. But I knew I needed to get a move on taking my life back while I still had one to take.

Gathering my strength, I focused on the things I could see and hear. Words began to take shape, becoming clearer, as did the images through my eyes.

Anabael was staring in a mirror, smiling. God, the sight of her contorting my face and wearing my skin like it was this season's latest fashion made me wish I could throw up. It was probably was a good thing I didn't have control of my arms and hands right now, as all I wanted to do was claw my own face off.

"There you are. I can feel you in there," she said, "wiggling around like a little worm."

Holy shit, she was talking to me.

"I have to admit, I thought you might have been different, but you're weak, just like all the rest, cowering in the back of your own mind like a little mouse. No, there is nothing special about you in the slightest, hunter."

Okay, Ev, ignore her and focus—what do you see? A white room, we are in a white room. Wait...I know this room. This was the bathroom back at the main house, my bathroom, the one I shared with Daniel, and I was wearing one of his old shirts.

She wanted me to fight? Fine, I'd give her a fucking fight. I gathered my strength and aimed everything I had into one point.

I heard Anabael hiss in pain and felt her press a hand to her left temple.

"Fuck, you little shit." In the reflection in the mirror I saw her brace her hands on the sink and stare deep into her own eyes, into me. The inner world around me began to quake as my focus slipped, and I felt myself buckle under the pressure. She was trying to push me out.

A good fighter knows when to back off and gather your strength, and if I didn't back off now, she was going to knock me down for the count.

It was good to know I could get through to her and cause her pain, but that wasn't going to be enough, not by a long shot. Before I pulled back completely and hunkered down in my little dark corner, I wanted her to know that I would not go quietly into the night. She wouldn't suspect a second blow this soon, which is precisely why I needed to hit her again. Pooling my focus one more time, I stabbed out into her mind, and I didn't even care where it went.

"Bitch!" she snarled, and I felt her body sag. Her head—my head—cracked on the side of the sink before she slipped to the floor. The movement of my own body felt strange. It almost felt like I was suspended in water inside my own skin but at the same time floating away on some weird currant. The sounds coming in through my ears grew more distant, what little light I could see beginning to dim.

No.

The echo of another voice penetrated the darkness—Isolde.

"Oh my goodness, Evelyn, I warned you not to get out of the bed unsupervised." I heard the panic in her voice, but only barely, because she sounded so quiet. Then she touched my arm. For some strange reason, when she made contact, it didn't feel muted as other physical sensations had. She felt solid, like she was touching *me*, not me through Anabael. Her voice became clear and crisp as well, as if she were sitting right next to me.

This must have been part of what Isolde and Lana had done to protect me. They'd known this would happen, and that I wouldn't be the one in charge of my arms, legs, and brain. And now Isolde was trying to make contact with me. Wasn't she?

It was the only thing I had to go on at this point. Time to test the theory.

Reaching out of my hiding place, I latched onto that feeling, took a hold of the line Isolde had thrown out to me, and held on for dear life. But how could I keep this connection without dropping my guard against Anabael?

Think, Evs. You're smart. Isolde knows it, and knows how your brain works. Think.

Technically, I had no physical body. That was being run by Bitchy Pants Demon Whore. So, the boundaries linked to the physical didn't exist for me, right? There was only one way to find out. I concentrated on the connection I had to Isolde right now, the virtual line she'd thrown me.

What if…

As I looked down, I saw that my consciousness had manifested into the form of the body I no longer controlled—my own body inside my *mind*, if that made any sense. And I was no longer latched on to what I'd perceived as Isolde's hand, but a length of rope. Nice. Looping the end around my "waist," I secured the line with one of those fancy knots Alex had taught me to tie ages ago. I now had my "hands" free. Okay, so it probably wasn't necessary to literally have both of my "hands" free—I guess I could have conjured up a third arm if I really wanted to—but keeping this as close as possible to reality helped me to focus.

I stared out into what was in essence my own psyche. I could almost see Anabael's stench all over it, slithering around my brain and turning my neural pathways into her own.

Fuck that shit.

But how the hell was I going to stop it?

Surely Isolde would have given me something else to latch on to other than herself; she wasn't so high and mighty that she would assume her presence alone would reach me. I touched the rope at my waist, my grounding line. Instantly, I felt more stable and sure. Then a slight noise rose behind me, and I turned around to see that something was tucked into the farthest corner of where I'd hidden myself. Moving closer, I saw a pair of boots come into view first—not just any boots. Daniel's boots. Of course…in working that spell, Isolde and Lana had managed to plant an image of Daniel into the back of my brain.

The darkness lifted enough for me to see him sitting in one of those rickety-ass folding chairs, leaning over with his elbows on his legs and hands dangling between his spread knees. That smile of his spread across his face, and his blue eyes lit with so much love my heart began to pound.

"You got this, babe," he said, nodding. "I don't know what *this* is exactly, but I know you, and you got this." He stood to his full height, all six-feet-two-inches of him—at least he appeared that tall in relation to my new "body." He walked over and took my face in his hands, then pressed his warm, sweet lips to mine. "*We* got this," he whispered before he was gone.

That was precisely what I needed. That one little bit of hope cloaked in a blanket of safety.

I turned to the highway of brain activity, stepped out of my little safe room, and bolted the door behind me. Tendrils of Anabael slid in and out of the folds of my brain like snakes.

There was only one way to see if this would work.

I took a deep breath, reached out, grabbed hold of one of the tails and pulled. There was tension, like it was trying to hold on to my mind. I probably could have just yanked the damned thing out, but it was slippery, just like Anabael. Besides, I was trying to be stealthy about this, and if I went into my own gray matter all gangbusters and shit, she'd feel it or sense it or something. Wrapping my hands around what I perceived to be a legless creature, I slowly worked it free until it flopped to the ground before me, snapping and snarling. I picked up my foot and slammed it back down on the head, crushing the thing with a crunch. The flopping stopped, and it lay there for a second before it shriveled up and turned to dust.

Well, that worked. Awesome. Now if I had a little more sumpin' sumpin', I could go at this with my bare hands, but it would be nice to have a weapon of some sort.

Almost as soon as the thought left my head, I felt the steel in my hands and weight on my shoulders, pulling down across my chest. Looking down, I saw a beautiful M16 in my hands and two bandoliers loaded with clips crisscrossed over my chest. This had to be Lana; as a newly retired hunter, she would have known I wanted something substantial. Now, normally I didn't go for such an ostentatious weapon, but in this case, it was perfect.

I stared out at the writhing mass that was my poor little possessed brain, hitched up my pants, and locked and loaded. This was an infestation, and I was the exterminator. Time to clean house.

CHAPTER 18
ANABAEL

Clearly this hunter wasn't going to give over her body as easily as I'd first thought. No matter, though; in fact, it was better. The inevitable surrender was always that much sweeter when the former inhabitant fought.

Isolde hummed irritatingly as she stitched the wound closed on my forehead.

"Where's Daniel?" I asked. "I haven't seen him at all since I've been home." He occupied quite a large portion of Evelyn's mind, and I was curious to see what the fuss was all about.

"He's out on assignment with Josie and Tony. As they say, no rest for the wicked. I assure you, the wicked ones never rest, and neither shall we. He should be back in a couple of days, though." She smiled and winked at me, and all I wanted to do was throttle her, squeeze the life out of her pretty little neck until the bones cracked. "There, that should do it. Now drink this."

"What is it?"

"Just a special little concoction of mine, something to help you rest and heal. You should be right as rain tomorrow."

I looked down at the opaque liquid in the cup and took a whiff.

"It smells like ass. What is with you and Tess? Can't you guys make something that doesn't smell and taste like a month-old jock strap?"

"You haven't even tasted it yet." She chuckled. Good, I'd answered with Evelyn's typical snark.

That little stunt Evelyn had pulled inside my head had taken its toll on my strength, though, and I had to be on my top game if I was going to overthrow the balance of power in this house. Whatever was in this potion would set my body back to top fighting form.

Tilting the cup to my lips, I winced at the foul flavor assaulting my mouth.

"I stand corrected, it tastes like a year-old jock strap that has been fermenting in the bottom of some sweaty dude's locker."

After Isolde left, I stretched in the bed, feeling this new skin slide over the powerful muscles inside of this body. The skin was quite lovely, really. It had been an age since I'd inhabited anyone this young; well, as young as she appeared, anyway. I could feel the experience pulsing deep inside her flesh — no, *my* flesh. This perfectly pale pink skin deliciously marked with such vibrant colors. The thought alone of how much pain she had to have endured for such extensive markings was intoxicating, to say the least. I imagined I could take on this world and the next in this body. Slay man, woman, child, *and* beast without raising a finger. Just one look from these blue eyes, and I'd have them all bending to my will, floating away in the oceanic depths.

My first plan of attack was inside this house. Break down the system from within these very walls. I closed my eyes and burrowed into Evelyn's temporal lobe, stealing into her hippocampus for any bit of memory I could use. More specifically, memories of men — the simplest of creatures, regardless of the species, and the easiest to turn. It had been nearly a hundred years since I'd lain with a man — or a woman, for that matter — and I was feeling a particular itch that needed to be scratched.

Flashes of men flickered behind my eyelids. One in particular, this Daniel fellow, seemed to be the star of the show. Very nice indeed, with skills in the bedroom that I could certainly appreciate. But he wouldn't be home for a few days. No matter, I had patience.

I'd all but decided that I would wait and make him my first mark until another memory danced through my consciousness…jealousy. There was a strain of jealousy between Daniel and another one of the male hunters in the house. A jealousy steeped in carnal knowledge of the very hunter's body I inhabited. Ahhh, nothing stirred the notorious pot more than pitting one green-eyed monster against the other.

I allowed the memory of Evelyn and a hunter named Zach take me to another place. He was a large man, nearly dwarfing that Daniel guy. Their sex was hot, raw, and animalistically glorious, and it seemed to have only happened the one time.

Now *that* was the very definition of a pity. I would rectify that very soon. With a smile, I ran my hands over my new body, glorying in its perfection and beauty.

I could still feel Evelyn's consciousness moving about inside my head, poking and prodding. It made the back of my eyes hurt and my temples burn, but that wouldn't last much longer. I pushed the pain aside, tamped it down and let the recognition of a night many years ago flood my system and reignite feelings of lust.

Even though I had not been born into a physical body, I was still female, and that part of me ached for a man's touch. There had been a time when that man was Lucifer, possibly the only thing I missed from being one of his treasured few. There was no need for a physical body when your lover was the devil himself. He could take me into his body and breathe me out in the most unholy manner that only he could achieve.

My own memories intermingled with those of the hunter, creating a new and decidedly debauched movie of wild and wanton fantasy. The glorious beauty that was Lucifer melded with the big beautiful being that was the hunter, Zach. Hell, I even allowed the images of Daniel to bleed through and join the madness. A delicious tangle of hairy male limbs, large hands, and hard lengths, groping, pulling, and caressing me and each other. My breath came out in a harsh gasp as the scenario grew to a fevered pitch and my eyes flew open.

Reality and the effects of the potion crashed down on me like a boulder as I took in the large bed I was in. White, stale, and so very lonely. I curled onto my side, drawing my knees up into my chest, and pulled the sheet tightly around me. The sensation was exquisitely uncomfortable, my new skin feeling too tight, the room feeling too small, and the fervor racing through my veins, and yet I denied myself any satisfaction, for it would come and it would be magnificent.

The next time I opened my eyes, I looked to the clock on the bedside table and saw that I had slept for a good ten hours. Reaching up to my forehead, I felt the wound was nearly healed from the salve Isolde had plastered on top of it after she'd sewn it closed. I stood from the bed, testing my new body by taking steps toward the bathroom. I was strong, my legs sure underneath me.

I cleansed myself in the shower before I moved to the medicine cabinet and found a pair of scissors. As I stood in front of the small mirror over the sink, I clipped the now loose stitches and pulled them free, leaving nothing but a thin pink line where the skin had split open.

Staring into the mirror, I tried to focus on the hunter, the little worm wiggling around inside my skull, biting and gnawing and twisting about. The pressure she created behind my eyes might have been unbearable in a lesser being, but she had no idea of the pain I could endure for my cause.

"You really think you can harm me, don't you?" I picked up the scissors and pressed the pointed end into the heel of my palm. Blood welled up around the stainless steel instrument. "Keep trying, please, I beg of you. More please, because I love it. I'm from Hell—I was born to pain."

The scissors clattered to the sink basin after I'd pulled them free. I curled my hand into a fist and dug my fingers into the open hole; pain skittered up my arm and away from my head, clearing my thoughts. I then rifled through the drawers next to the sink and found a gauze bandage to slap over the open wound.

As I smoothed the tape down, my demon senses picked up a scent that had drifted under the closed bathroom door behind me—a male scent—and the wanton desires of sex resurfaced, hotter and more powerful than the night before. This could no longer wait. After over a hundred years of celibacy, the carnal need inside of me had been unleashed. The takeover would begin now.

"Evie," a voice asked with a knock. "Are you okay in there? You want me to get Tess or Isolde for you?"

My mouth practically watered with need. Flinging the door open, my gaze moved up the hard body standing before me, and I took in that big, beautiful animal of a lover…the hunter, Zach.

His eyes widened as he stood staring at my naked body, which still glistened from the shower.

"Whoa…um, sorry, I…I'll leave." He blinked rapidly and yet never looked away.

"No," I said as I reached out and grabbed the waistband of his jeans, pulling him closer. "You're just what I need."

He swallowed hard when I stretched onto my tiptoes and licked the pulsing vein in his neck. "We…we can't do this."

"Why? Don't you want this?" My hand drifted down over his hard length. "Clearly you do, and so do I. See?" I took his hand in mine and slid it between my legs, letting him feel the wetness there. Lucifer, it felt so good to be wet again.

"Jesus, Ev," he groaned, lightly biting his bottom lip, his finger fluttering for a moment before he pulled away. "No, I'm not doing this. Daniel—"

"Isn't here, and you are." I worked his belt open. "I think about you." Pushing past the barrier of his boxers, I gripped his length. "I think about this big, hard cock and how good it was."

"Fuck," he said under his breath.

"Yes, we did, like writhing animals. Hot, sweaty animals fucking until we couldn't move anymore. Don't you miss that? Don't you miss what we had?"

His entire body stiffened and his hands came down on my shoulders, shoving me away.

"We didn't have anything, Ev."

"Fine," I growled. "I was going to let you fuck me stupid, but clearly we are going to have to do this my way."

"What does that mean?"

Pulling on spells stored in Evelyn's memory banks, I raised my palms. "*Kef 'oc b'crol!*" I watched as the energy I summoned radiated out of my open palms and knocked him off his feet. He landed right where I wanted him, in the center of the bed.

I peeled off his shirt, then grabbed the legs of his jeans and ripped them off his body. While he struggled with consciousness, I fished out four strong leather belts from the dresser and tied him to the wrought iron bed frame.

As he came around, I slid up his body and stuck my mouth to his. He tasted like the most delicious sin. Pushing my clit against his half-hard cock, I rejoiced as it started swelling back to life.

"Please, stop this," he begged through gritted teeth, straining against the bonds.

"Yes," I moaned. In this virile body and after so many chaste years, I needed little more than this external contact to near climax. If he would only plead again, perhaps cry, that would push me over the edge. Even just the thought made me wetter.

I slipped over him until his tip caught in my wet, ready opening. Tilting my hips, I reached down and held him straight to finally sink down on him when a searing pain shot through the back of my head and I was lifted off and flung across the room before I could feel him inside of me.

The one called Lana stood between me and my prize. Stark, blond beauty. Lust ripped through me at the rage coming off of her. The urge to taste anything and everything boiled my control, and I panted with craving.

"Don't be so jealous, darling," I said. "There is more than enough of that cock for the both of us, and then we can have each other."

Her fist connected with my jaw, cracking my head back and knocking me to the ground. The coppery taste of blood filled my mouth. It was good. I sucked on the flavor and rolled it around. I could feel it on my teeth as I smiled up at her and got to my feet, spitting a mouthful of blood onto the floor.

"I'll take that as a no."

Strong hands gripped my arms from behind, pulling me up straight. Pain burst in my body as I struggled against my captor, and it made me laugh. I felt hot breath at my ear and smelled sweet peppermint, a scent this body knew. Daniel.

"Honey, you're home. Why don't you join us? I'm sure Z gives amazing head." I hissed as he pulled my body tight, even though it didn't really hurt. So he *wasn't* on assignment; the other hunters likely weren't either. This had all been a ruse. They'd known I would come here as Evelyn and had given me a false sense of security to catch me off-guard. A small part of me admired that level of deceit.

Writhing, I twisted to try to look Daniel in the face, which forced him to tighten his hold even further.

"Mmm, that's good."

"Stop it." He pulled the sheet off of the bed and wrapped it around me. "We know who you are."

"Really now? Then let me enlighten you…she wishes you'd do that more, pull her hair and show her what a real man can do. Did you know that when I took over, I showed her what fun we could have with men, the hearty male slaves she could have at her disposal, and she loved every single second of it. The way they could fill her up. She's a dirty little beast. Deep down, all women are, really. She especially enjoyed the idea of anal play, and I truly believe she would give as good as she got."

With every word that spilled from my mouth, I watched sweet little Daniel's rage build until it spilled over, just like I wanted it to. That one spark, that one little glimmer of doubt in his eyes—and there it was, the tiniest of flickers. Time to fan the flames.

"I don't believe a word, she wouldn't let you—"

"Honey, did you forget what you walked in on? I wish I could say that it was all me, but her memory of Zach in the sack plays over and over in my mind. I can hardly escape it. So I might have initiated the seduction, but once things heated up, she couldn't wait to get him inside of her. Clearly my body has a memory, too."

"This isn't your body, bitch," he growled as he gave me a good, hard shake. "Consider this your eviction notice. Get your fucking ass out of my girlfriend and you might live."

"You don't seem to get it. You can't have her. What's left of your precious little girlfriend is mine—her body, mind, and soul. And even if by some miracle of a chance you manage to wrench me free of this body, I assure you, darling, I am going to shred every last ounce of her pathetic little soul before I depart from it. Your dear sweet Evelyn is dead!"

CHAPTER 19
EVELYN

I immersed myself in the task of ridding my cerebral cortex of Anabael, even though the task seemed daunting as all hell. Every time I vanquished one of her demon eels, two or three more would pop up in its place. I was sweaty and exhausted and almost out of ammo. Not to mention, a couple of those gnarly critters almost took a hunk out of my ass before I could squash it.

I tried to stay focused on getting my mind free—but then she started with Z. Teasing and taunting him with my body. Jesus.

Part of me wanted to curl up in a ball and cry. Full on, snot-sobbing, gut-wrenching, ugly crying. I didn't even know if I was actually accomplishing anything here anyway. Maybe this wasn't doing a damn thing and all I'd achieved was weakening myself, and that's why she'd been able to abuse Z the way she had.

Great. Doubt was the last thing I needed to deal with right now.

I doubled over, panting. The virtual muscles in my virtual arms ached as I pushed my wet hair out of my face with hands that shook like an old woman's.

Then it hit me: I *was* an old woman. A one-hundred-and-thirty-five-year-old woman.

Visions flashed through my mind, crawling through my brain like cockroaches. Images manifested themselves before my eyes, as if the picture was being projected onto the inside of my skull like some perverse mirror.

I looked at my trembling hands. They were gnarled, veins bulging and the skin so paper-thin that I could practically see the tendons underneath. My hair morphed, becoming dull, white, and half the thickness it had been before. When I tried to straighten to my full height, my body wouldn't cooperate, the bones and muscles screaming with pain and refusing to move.

What the hell? My true age was barreling down on me like a goddamned freight train.

"This can't be happening." My inner voice sounded tired, used up until it was nothing more than a scratchy semblance of what it once was.

Another voice echoed around me, a sick, evil one—Anabael's.

"Evelyn, sweet, darling little Evelyn, I know what you're doing in there. Well, what you're trying to do. It won't work, by the way, and quite frankly, I'm tiring of this nonsense. You had to have seen the fun I've been having with your body. That Z is quite the little boy toy. And Daniel? Did you see his face when I told him that fucking Z was your desire, too? I'm surprised he didn't break down right there like a girl."

"You lied."

"I'm the liar? Come now, don't you think I can't feel your guilt? What's the matter, Evelyn, did I touch on a sore spot, or do you simply feel guilty that he was hurt by what you did?"

"What *you* did, Anabael. I had no part of that."

"Let's not get caught up in technicalities. Besides, you're forgetting I know your fears, your deepest, darkest fears. You are afraid that Daniel will finally grow bored at the novelty of you, a woman so many years his senior. But don't worry, I've covered that. You see, if by chance you happen to get rid of me, you may still have your eternal life, but I will take your precious youth with me. You'll be nothing but a wrinkled, twisted up old woman. Do you think your beloved Daniel will want you then?"

I looked around and saw the demon snakes swirling around the door where my love for Daniel was hidden, biting at the steel, bending it back at the edges. I tried to move, only to find even more of the snakes twisted around my ankles, rooting me to the ground.

"No," I croaked as I fought against their hold.

Anabael's cackle ricocheted off the inside of my skull. "I will hand it to you, it was very clever to attempt to conceal him away from me. Very clever indeed. But you should have known that you can't hide anything from me. Nothing."

That's when it happened.

A sudden jolt rocked through my actual my body. A delicious arc of energy that was oh-so familiar, and then his voice broke through the madness.

"I know you're in there, baby. I know it in my bones. You fight that bitch; you fight her with everything you've got!"

My back snapped straight and my muscles began to strengthen.

I felt myself propel forward, and yet I hadn't moved an inch inside the corner of my mind. I looked out the portholes of my physical eyes and saw the basement hallway breeze past me. The inside of the infirmary came into view for a moment as the sensation of being pulled down and picked up at the same time overtook me.

I panicked for a moment before I realized that it was my body, my tangible body, being lifted up and laid prone. What was happening to me? I was feeling more of my actual self…but how?

As I looked out over the expanse of my brain, I noticed something. The evil eel-snake things I'd been fighting were nearly gone, as if the second my ears had heard Daniel's voice and my skin felt his touch, a veil had been lifted. The grotesque image Anabael had planted into my subconscious had all but vanished.

Another jolt rocked my body, but this one was different, more violent, and it took a second to realize that I'd been hurled—not too gently—onto an exam table. My arms and legs were pulled out straight and bound at the wrist and ankles.

"Let me go!" I heard myself say, my body bucking against the restraints.

They'd been *her* words, her actions, not mine. Yet in that moment, tied to the table, an ancient memory came rushing back, one where I was lashed to a very different sort of exam table in a very different sort of room. Agnews, The Great Asylum for the Insane. That was the place where my parents had taken me to "fix" me before marrying me off to some weirdo who'd have been okay with me being a little eccentric. But that hadn't been good enough for my father; he'd feared the engagement would fall through if this clown learned the true extent of my insanity. I couldn't blame them, really; we'd been coming up on the turn of the twentieth century, and what else would they do with someone who said they saw demons—especially a girl from a family near the top of the social ladder. I'd been trapped in that place for two years before Alex and Isolde had found me, broken down, tortured by the demons that masked themselves as nurses and orderlies, and terrified that the next session to "cure" me would be the one that finally ended me.

Pure terror shot through me at the mere thought of another ice bath or some other ungodly fresh hell the nurses had found for me, and I unleashed a blood-curdling scream.

Me.

From my own mouth.

The next second, Tess was in my field of vision, her soft hands on my face.

"There you are," she said. "You had me scared for a second. I was about ready to crawl in there with you and drag your ass out."

"You gotta untie my hands and feet, Tess. I can't fight like this. It's too much like before—" my voice turned into a terrified whisper "—in there, in that place."

"I know, honey. Believe me, if there is anyone in this room who knows what you went through in that hellhole, it's me. But there isn't any other way. She's still in there with you, and we can't risk—"

"You fucking bitch," I snarled through my lips, and Tess only laughed in response. She knew damn well those words weren't mine.

"Like I was saying, we can't risk Demon Von Whoreslut rearing her skanky little head again."

"Demon Von Whoreslut, nice."

I watched the ceiling panels pass through my field of vision as my head turned, and I saw Tony saunter into the room with Josie. Warmth blossomed along the length of the tattoo that bound us all as a team, and I could feel the sensation as mine, not as an echo of what Anabael was feeling on my skin.

"You will never reclaim this body," she snarled, and an evil cackle ripped out of my throat, spraying my lips with spittle. "If you so much as think about removing me from this body, I will drag her back to Hell, and she will live out the rest of eternity as Lucifer's own personal plaything."

A leather strap tightened against my wrist, and I was cognizant that the feeling was secondary, that once again Anabael was in control. My time driving the flesh machine that was my own body had disappeared almost as quickly as it had surfaced.

Daniel's fingers brushed my wrist. I knew it was his touch because I could feel it as my skin, and it felt right and true; only he could touch me like that. And just as before, I felt a stronger hold inside of my body.

This wasn't going to be easy, though. I would have to not only fight the demon trying to take over my life, but tied down to this gurney, I'd have to fight a completely different set of demons as well. Ones I'd been fighting for over a hundred years. Ones that I'd thought I had a handle on. Ones that could very well be the only handle I had to grab on to at the moment.

Well, these and Daniel. All my years on this planet, I'd always felt that I'd been searching for something, something that seemed just out of my reach. I had ignorantly assumed that something was my work as a hunter. It was what I was born to do, who I was born to be. My life was complete and whole, at least that's what I had told myself. Then Daniel had sauntered in. From the moment I'd seen him, as much as I hadn't wanted to admit it at the time, I'd known he was what had been missing. His absence was what had kept me from being the best hunter I could possibly be. But I had that now. I had him, his love and devotion, and he had mine. It was a thing, a tangible, palpable thing that anyone could see and feel; it was like the cosmos vibrated with joy because we were together.

As if he could sense my need to see him, to strengthen the connection between my soul and his, he moved into my field of vision. His shirt was off and he looked…different. Fresh tattoos covered his chest, up over his shoulders, down over his taut belly and swept into the piece on his back. Each arm was covered in ink, deep blue scrollwork that illuminated an almost neon candescence.

His hand gripped the bill of a ball cap he had on. Odd, he'd never been one for hats before. But when he swept the green cap off of his head, I could feel the air rush out of my body in a gasp.

All of his hair, every single strand, was gone, shaved down to the skin. In its place were ancient symbols, incantations, and most surprisingly, my name. Over and over again, in between every spell, wound around each marking.

Dear God, this might actually work.

CHAPTER 20
DANIEL

After pulling Anabael off of Z, I'd tried to push her out of the room and into the hallway by myself, but her feet dragged against the floor. She'd gone completely limp, like all the fight had gone out of her. Z picked up her other side after Lana untied him, and together we moved her down the hallway, through the kitchen, and down the basement stairs into the infirmary—all while trying to keep that damn sheet on her.

Carefully, we hoisted her up to lay her on the gurney. Her body twisted in midair, struggling against us, so we had to manhandle her down onto the table. As carefully as we could manage, we held her limbs out straight while Tess and Lana, who had followed us into the room, secured her arms and legs.

"Let me go!" she screamed as her body arched off the table. She fought hard, wrenching herself this way and that with such violence I had to look away. I wanted to back away altogether, to run as far as I could to get away from what I'd just seen in the other room.

Evie, on top of Z, sliding her body up and down on his, her fingers wrapped around her breasts, head thrown back in pleasure. I knew what she looked like when she was about to lose it, when she was about to...Jesus, I couldn't even think it. The image was burned into my brain, etched into the backs of my eyeballs so deep that I still saw it when I closed my eyes.

How do you wash something like that away?

Isolde's last words before she had left came back to me, clawing through the vile image into the more rational part of my mind.

"Remember, when you see Evelyn, she will not be in control of her body. Anabael will be. She will sense the bond you have with her, and she will exploit it, make Evelyn do things, especially if she perceives that it is going to drive a wedge between the two of you. Do not let it. You must be strong and trust in what you feel in your heart, not what you see with your eyes."

I looked across the table at Z, who had Evie's other wrist and leg pinned down. He still wasn't wearing a shirt, but at least he'd taken a second to put his pants back on. I'd wanted to strangle him, to leap on top of him while he was still strapped to that bed, *my* bed, and beat the ever-loving shit out of him. I would have done it, too; truth be told, I was still half-considering doing just that after everything was said and done.

I was planning the whole thing out when his eyes met mine. He shook his head and looked away, as if he couldn't bear to look at me.

I'm sorry, he mouthed when he finally turned back. I replayed the image in my head again and tried to focus on him. The look on his face, the revulsion, the way he'd twisted his body and tried to free himself. His body may have responded when he'd been forced to participate—a guy's body is going to react to being touched even if he doesn't want it to—but he hadn't enjoyed that encounter with Evie...Anabael. At least, he hadn't appeared to. So I had to feel bad for him. Strapped to a bed and forced into sex, let alone with the body of a woman he would have done anything to have under any other circumstances.

I saw Alex standing in the doorway, the other members of the house huddled behind him. He looked like hell. Dark circles ringed his eyes, and he'd lost some weight, which made him look older.

Looking over all the faces that I could see, I saw the same thread of worry and sorrow, the same worn-out appearance, like the life force was being sucked out of them slowly. I guess it was. They were all tied to Evie, too, through the charm that linked our strength to hers.

Isolde placed a hand on Alex's shoulder as she moved in behind him. Normally she wouldn't have a hair out of place, but the train had jumped the normal track in the last week, hadn't it? She smiled reassuringly at me as she slipped around him to enter the room, and I was reminded of another moment we'd had together before she'd left to collect Evie.

"You may come to a point where you want to give up. You may even wonder if there is any part of Evelyn in there to save. She may not be able to give you any kind of sign that her soul still exists. This is when it is most important to dig in and not give up. When all seems lost is usually when the light shines through. And when it happens, and I know that it will, remember that the softest brush of skin on skin between two people who love each other can reach through the densest fogs."

This had to be that time, because I was desperate at this point. I would have done anything for a glimmer of the woman I knew, the woman I loved. I'd have swallowed my pride and begged on my hands and knees to save her, and if I couldn't, I'd pray for the strength to do what was needed. To give up. To find the closest weapon and end the madness. I would do that for her if I felt there wasn't any other option, and we were rapidly approaching that decision.

That was when I heard it. The most wonderful sound I'd ever heard. An eardrum-splitting, blood-curdling scream so loud and primal that we all stopped what we were doing and stared.

"There you are," Tess said, getting right down to her face. She stroked her cheeks and smoothed her hair back, speaking to a part of Evie that I didn't know.

I started to move, to take over because it should be me talking to her. We were bonded.

Isolde caught me by the arm and shook her head. "No, this is not your part," she whispered into my ear, so quietly only I could hear. "She isn't properly restrained. You must finish binding her. Tess doesn't have the strength to hold her down like you do."

I felt tears prickle at the backs of my eyes as Evie begged to be free. Evie. I knew it was her. I could tell by the sound of her voice.

But in the next instant, Anabael was back, spouting hate and vileness. Closing my eyes, I looped the leather strap around her arm and pulled it tight, letting my fingers graze the inside of her wrist. She turned her head and I saw her—Evie—almost as if she was peeking out from behind the demon's cold, soulless glare. I nodded to her with a soft smile before I stepped completely out of her sight.

Right. Time to get this show on the road, I thought as I unbuttoned my shirt and let it fall to the floor.

CHAPTER 21
ANABAEL

Daniel. His bond to Evelyn was extremely strong, and it seemed to grow stronger. And no wonder—that sneaky little shit had bound himself to her. Just look at him with her name scrawled all over his body. On his head, for fuck's sake.

I had to crack whatever held the two of them together and get into his mind, into that plane of doubt that every man had.

I spoke softly, but not so quietly that only Daniel could hear.

"You know, when I was on top of Z, riding him with this body, I saw what your Evelyn truly felt for him. Oh yes, her body responded like a woman who had already had a taste of that big, hard dick. We got wet, so wet for that cock, and when we felt it sliding in and out of us, it felt so fucking good to be filled with it again. It's much bigger than yours, did you know that? God, you probably don't even know that she fakes it when she's with you just so she can go lock herself in the bathroom and finger bang herself while thinking of him."

"That is quite enough."

The voice that came from the doorway was familiar from my own memories. So proper and crisp it could only have only come from one person in this house.

Alexander.

"Well, well, well, if it isn't the root of Evelyn's Electra Complex. I'm sure you know how many twisted fantasies she harbors for you. Surely you must. A big, strong, handsome *older* man swooping in to save her from the evil institution her real father put her in. Tell me, does she call you 'daddy' when you fuck her?"

I saw rage in Alexander's eyes as his lip twitched and his jaw clenched tight. We both knew he'd never laid a finger on Evelyn's body no matter who was inside it—he wouldn't dream of it—but I could tell he itched to drop his stern, composed exterior and lash out at me for suggesting such a thing even if it marred his precious Princess Evelyn's flesh.

Members of the house filed in, carrying trays, small tables, and stools. They placed a candle on top of each one as they set them down in a circle around the gurney. No one spoke or even looked in my direction.

The next voice I heard caused my body to snap taut. Isolde had entered, her eyes gleaming with power as she quietly began to recite an incantation.

"Witch," I spat, straining against the leather straps. I pulled on Evelyn's strength spells, summoning them with my will. I would break these bindings with the magic and strength I felt coursing through her body.

I jerked as hard as I could against the restraints, expecting them to all but obliterate into nothingness, only for them to hold fast. Bucking on the table, I tried again, shouting the spell at the top of my lungs to bring forth as much power as I possibly could. Still, I was lashed to the cursed table.

"It is of no use," Alexander said. "The table and the bindings are spelled to counteract any possible strength incantation."

Isolde's chanting filled the room. Every candle exploded to light, and the spoken words started to sink in.

S'dhyeth nisk mor f'when ec niht aere nihiw't.

No. She, of all people could *not* know this spell. No one outside of the fifth level of Hell even knew it existed.

Something shifted inside of Evelyn's body. No, not something… me, myself, moving and slipping within this flesh, against her bones. It began to feel too cramped, like I was being pushed to the surface.

"How do you know these words?" I grunted and struggled harder to get free.

"I told her, my dear." The new voice I heard was sultry and sweet, the most wonderful voice in all the world.

My vision was murky, but I didn't need my sight to know whose voice I was hearing. The shape of a man took form on the other side of the room.

"Hello, child," Lucifer said with a smile as his face came into focus.

Pure panic pulsed inside of me. "Master," I gasped.

"Mmmm, yes, so you do remember that I am your master. I was wondering because it seems as if you'd forgotten, what with your running about the earthly plane, trying to bring an unholy end to the world and all. You know, one might even perceive that as a threat, if one was inclined to be threatened. Luckily for you, I am not so inclined, especially from beings so weak and inadequate that they can't even seem to manifest their own bodies."

As he spoke he strolled closer, looming in like the very meaning of the word *sinister*.

"Master, you misunderstand. I do this all for you, to honor you—"

"Lies," he whispered. That was his way. He wouldn't bellow at the top of his lungs; he would lean in close to your ear and speak only to you. His cold breath raked across my skin when he spoke, and I both loved it and feared it. "In all the centuries you have been in my service, you have known the pleasures of my domain, the wondrous, carnal delights that await those who might find themselves in my good graces."

The memories of his gloriously sinful body flooded over me. The endless sessions of hot, sweaty sex I'd had with Lucifer inside of nearly every body I had inhabited, even when I'd happened to inhabit the body of a man. Sometimes, that in and of itself had been the best part. I wanted to hate him, wanted to spurn him, to spit my loathing for him and his power at him with everything inside of me, but I couldn't. Not with him standing over me, taunting me in that magnificent way he had. He would always have a hold on me; I realized that now. I would always belong to him, and I hated myself for it.

"You are remembering, aren't you?" His cool tongue flicked out to stroke my earlobe.

"Yes, master," I breathed.

"Good, I want you to remember. It is my wish that you remember every moment you felt love and adoration from me, for it will never happen again."

My throat closed up.

"If you will recall, my realm is Hell, and you shall know every possible meaning of that. There will be no pleasure. Even in the pain, you will not know a moment of rest. And when you are broken and can't take another moment, I will start anew, and you will remember that *I* am Lucifer and I will not be made a fool of."

Someone's hand settled on my abdomen. It was large and seemed to sear right through my skin as a voice assaulted my ears, so sweet and melodic that it could only be that of the angel I despised with all of my being — Gabriel.

"S'dhyeth nisk mor f'when ec niht aere nihiw't," Gabriel murmured as he moved his hand in a circular motion.

"No, no, no!" I thrashed. "You can't let them do this to me!"

"My dear, you did this to yourself," Lucifer whispered before he took a step back. His green eyes that had once gazed upon me with such virility and fire now pierced me with their cold loathing.

The sensation of Gabriel's hand on my essence forced an inhale that I could not release. My eyes widened in horror as I saw his elbow bend, drawing me out of this body. I latched on to the flesh, tried to grab hold of anything I could to remain in this human vessel.

"S'dhyeth nisk mor f'when ec niht aere nihiw't."

The arms of my host body quivered and the skin of her abdomen puckered, tenting up and turning purple against the pull.

"S'dhyeth nisk mor f'when ec niht aere nihiw't!"

Gabriel's voice echoed off the walls of the small room as he jerked his arm back, and I was suddenly gazing down upon the hunter's body, the flesh of her stomach discolored from bruising but flat once again. Her lithe legs and graceful arms were slack and at rest against the gurney.

Contained within Gabriel's grasp, I had an odd sense of safety, the only time I'd ever had such a feeling save for while in the embrace of Lucifer.

That sensation would be short-lived.

"Anabael of the Simzahnomon Province," Gabriel said as my Spectoral essence twisted in his hold, "for your crimes against humanity and the balance of all things good and evil, I banish you from this plane of existence and return you to your maker to punish you as he sees fit. May Lucifer have mercy on you."

"I wouldn't count on that." Lucifer approached with a small clear jar in his hands. When the lid lifted, I felt myself being sucked down into the opening, crammed into the confines of what would surely be my eternal prison.

The moment the lid sealed, I saw through the glass that we were in Lucifer's lair, deep within the bowels of Hell. With a wave of his hand, a shallow opening appeared in the brimstone wall, just large enough for my container to sit. He stroked the side of my jar, and for a moment I thought he might show me mercy.

"I could remove you and torture you with any number of devices that have proved to be effective on your kind." The sinister smile that was once so appealing I now saw for the frightening sight it was. "I could drop a number of horrors inside there with you and let them drive you mad, and maybe when I grow bored I will. But for now I've chosen something that I know will be most torturous. I will do nothing. I know that may sound lenient at the moment, but when I say nothing, I mean nothing. I will not spare you a glance, a fleeting thought, or even a satisfied smile when I hear you screaming and begging to be set free. You will sit on this shelf and watch the world happen around you, for I know that there is no worse torture for a Spectoral as that of being unable to interact with another creature."

With another pass of his hand, the stone closed around me, sealing my jar into the wall though I could see through it as if it wasn't there. Everywhere I looked from within my tiny prison, I saw different things…levels of Hell, rooms within Lucifer's lair, the outside world in every realm of reality imaginable. All right there before me, but utterly out of my grasp.

Dear God, please have mercy on me.

CHAPTER 22
DANIEL

Evie's arms and legs stretched out at a forty-five degree angle from the table. I watched Gabriel pull the ghostly demon from her body, the spectral creature writhing in his grasp, and saw her limbs flop to the table as the blackness closed in around me. Lucifer held a jar aloft and turned to give me one last wink before he vanished and I slipped to the floor.

I blinked to clear my blurry vision. When I opened my eyes, I was sitting on the bunk in my dorm room at the University of Indianapolis. This is where Gabriel had recruited me and my handler/roommate Chris. Had everything that had happened in the last year and a half or so *not* happened?

"Hello, Daniel."

I looked up and saw Gabriel sitting on the bunk across from me, his legs crossed at the knee.

"Uh." Glancing around, I caught sight of my arms, and there was not a single drop of ink on them. I raised my hands to my scalp and felt a full head of hair. "What's going on?"

He rested his hands on his bent knee. "I'm giving you an opportunity."

"Right…" Confusion washed over me. "I thought we had this conversation. You offered me a position as a hunter with the Lebriga Corporation and I accepted. I became a hunter, didn't I?"

"Oh, you did. You are an excellent hunter and quite the addition to Alexander and his team. However, this is still very early on in your service, and when something like this happens, we like to give our young ones a second chance."

"'Kay, but I still don't get it. When something like what happens?"

"Well, Daniel, it seems as though this last assignment has placed you in a very precarious position." Gabriel stood and strode to the window, his hands clasped behind his back, and he released what I could only call an exasperated sigh. "You are what we call 'between.' You have the unique opportunity to…refresh. We will allow you to go back to the life you led before you accepted our offer and live it out as you would have had you declined."

"Hang on, so everything in the last year and a half *did* happen. I'm not tripping on some newfangled party drug someone slipped into my beer, am I?"

"No," he chuckled.

"Okay, so if that was real and you're real, then Evelyn and what we had was real?"

"Yes." He nodded.

"And if I go back to the way it was, back to being a regular Joe, all of that goes away?"

"I'm afraid so. If you choose to take your life back, it will be as if you'd never met. You will have no memory of her or anyone within the corporation."

"As if you'd never met."

Those five words hung in the air, hovering in the space between Gabriel and myself.

"You will have a life," he said, "a family."

If we'd never met, I would never have seen that moment of Evie and Z together. I would never have seen that spark of pleasure I'd caught in his eyes. Yeah, he'd been revolted by the demon, but it was still Evelyn's body, and I knew that deep down there was the smallest part of him that had enjoyed what was happening. He'd finally gotten what he'd wanted for so long, to be with her like that, the way they had before. So if we'd never met, I'd never have to live knowing—no, *seeing* he'd been with her…inside of her. I wouldn't see it every time I closed my eyes. That could all go away. Forever.

My chest clenched and my lips started to tingle.

"You'll finish school and go on to be a quite lucrative businessman."

If we'd never met, I would never have to hear the sounds she'd made as she rode on top of him. I would never have to look at her and wonder if there was any truth to the guttural moans of pleasure I'd known so well. Was there a part of her that had enjoyed it?

I felt a soft breeze blow across my face, my head, warming me to my toes.

"You will return to your hometown, where you will reunite with Meagan and have the life you had always imagined. You will move into a house in the same neighborhood you grew up in, and you will have three children together."

If we'd never met, I could be normal. Live a normal life, not just for a few minutes here and there when we could manage to squeeze it into our demon-hunting schedule. I'd have a house in the suburbs and be so blissfully normal with my wife and kids. I'd live the dream my parents had had for me.

Truthfully, I'd always wanted to be a father. When I'd imagined my life growing up, children had always been a part of that imagery. The ability to reproduce was one of the things we gave up when we became hunters, though, so to have biological children, I would have to choose my old life.

But those kids would be with Meagan, normal vanilla Meagan. Not Evelyn. Not fly-by-the-seat-of-her-pants, you-never-know-what's-going-to-come-out-of-her-mouth, tighten-your-seat-belt-because-we're-going-for-a-crazy-ride Evelyn. She would be gone, surgically removed from my mind, from my heart, from my very soul. Would I even have a soul without her?

Gabriel said all of those things would happen, but he'd never once mentioned that I would be happy. I couldn't help but wonder if a part of me would always grieve for Evie because I'd feel her void without knowing she even existed. Would mourning something I'd never had send me on a ruthless quest for success? I wondered if that part of me would always be looking for Evie and, in doing that, would never find happiness with anyone else. It could turn me into an adulterer, a shitty husband, and as a result of that, a wretched father who couldn't wait to be away from his kids.

But would Evie and I ever have what we had before the demon had taken over? What if that was gone, broken beyond repair? Would I wonder about her and Z every time I saw the two of them together, imagine them twisted together in various sexual positions? God, could I even look at her the same way again? Wouldn't it be better to have never seen it at all?

They say it's better to have loved and lost than never to have loved at all, but was that really the case?

Another completely different scenario popped into my head.

Was she even alive?

"Why are you doing this to me?" I asked. I felt confined, squelched.

"Nothing is being done to you, Daniel. This is a choice. Free will, remember? That's how contracts work in my business."

"But I don't have all the facts. I can't make a decision without all of the facts. I don't even know if she's still alive. That's not fair," I pled.

"*Fair* isn't in the contract, Daniel. You must choose, weigh your options."

Maybe all of this was for naught and I'd go back to live out the rest of eternity alone. The last memory of the woman I lived for wasn't of her with me but with another man. Did all the other days and nights, all the love we shared, weigh out that one blip in time? Did I risk it or did I play it safe and take the human life?

One thing niggled in the back of my brain…what if she made it out alive?

"Would she remember me? If I choose not to go back and she is alive, will she remember me?"

"Yes."

My lungs burned again, and something occurred to me—that this entire time sitting here with Gabriel, I had thought I'd been breathing. I mean, I was talking, wasn't I? How can I be breathing and still feel like I hadn't taken a breath? Closing my eyes, I let my lungs fill with air.

"Ah, I see you have made your choice."

CHAPTER 23
EVELYN

When my eyes opened, I was standing, yet I couldn't feel the floor underneath me. Odd thing was, I didn't feel like I was floating either.

If that wasn't bad enough, everything around me was white. It was like I was just stuck in the middle of the color white itself. Fucking odd.

As I turned to get a look around, I was more than slightly startled to find two men in suits standing behind me, staring like…like they knew me. One had golden hair that hung just past the shoulders of his scarlet jacket; the ends of the blond ringlets tickled the collar of his powder blue dress shirt, one lock nearly making it all the way to the perfectly tied peach tie. The man next to him, however, had rich brown hair that spilled down the back of his honey-colored suit in mahogany waves. They were both so impeccably dressed and utterly perfect that they could only remind me of one person on this planet…Gabriel.

Oh, shit.

"I'm dead, aren't I?" I asked, surprised to find my voice trembling when it came out of my mouth.

The two men didn't say a word. They just stood there looking all tall and powerful, ogling me like I was a science experiment they were observing and waiting for me to sprout a second head.

The backs of my eyes started to burn, and I could feel the tears build. Jesus, I always assumed I'd die in the line of duty at some point. I half-expected it every time I walked out of the door to take the next assignment. Hell, if I was being honest, I freaking welcomed it. At least I had before.

Now, though? I had finally found someone who made me want to *keep* living. Not that I'd had a death wish before, but with Daniel in my life, I had something that put the fear of death in me, which I'd never had before. These days I felt like I'd finally started living after merely existing.

"No." I shook my head vehemently. Looking from one man to the next and back again, I said, "Not yet, I'm not done." A near-psychotic laugh bubbled out of me before I could stop it. "You know what? Screw this noise. I refuse to be dead. Do you hear me? I'm not dying and you can't make me. There, now you have to send me back, you—" My throat closed around the rest of my words. Gathering myself, I finally managed to squeak out, "I *need* to go back."

Images flashed around me, filling the white void with snapshots of my life. My early days as a hunter, sparring with Alex. Close calls out in the field when I probably should have been killed but managed to escape by the skin of my teeth. Every member of the house as they entered my world, tilting it on its axis in a new way with each one. What they meant to me. Isolde patching me up, time and again. Tess driving me batshit and pushing the limits of what I was comfortable with emotionally.

And Daniel.

His image consumed all of the others until it was only him. His face, his smile, his laugh, his touch, his strength, the way he pushed my limits in a completely different respect. He opened me to the world in a way that I didn't think was even remotely possible for someone as old and set in their ways as I was. He was my saving grace in more ways than I could count. His love made me whole. I simply could not leave this life until I did the same for him to the best of my abilities. Period.

"I'm not done," I begged. "Please." Unbelievable. Me. The chick that didn't beg or plead for anything in her life; not even when my own parents had locked me away in that hospital had I uttered one word. But here, in this void that I could only assume was something between my world and the next, with tears streaming down my face, hiccupping like an idiot, I would beg my ass off for just one more day to show Daniel how much he meant to me. He would want me back, wouldn't he? Even after the shit Anabael had done with my body? Fuck it, he was getting me back whether he wanted me or not. "If you don't send me back, I'll find Lucifer and I'll get him to bring me back. I swear I will."

The men looked at each other and smiled as if they'd read my thoughts.

"Gabriel was right about this one. She is quite feisty," the one with the golden hair said.

"Yes, Michael, indeed," the other man said. "The question is, what do we do now?"

"Clearly we must do as Gabriel has asked, Raphael." Michael turned to me with a twinkle in his eye. "Send her back."

The world came rushing back with a jolt, like lightning had just coursed through my veins. With a gasp, I opened my eyes and sucked in great lungsful of air.

I was staring at something white again, but it wasn't like the void. This was something I knew all too well—the ceiling of the infirmary. I'd been in there enough to have memorized the layout of each mark and paint chip ten times over. Gabriel stood next to me, one of his great hands pressed to my chest, right over my heart. When he pulled back, I sat up so fast that the room around me tilted and spun on an invisible axis. I felt strange. Like my skin was filled with a billion more nerve endings and stretched way too tight. Everything was too loud, too bright, too…everything. I felt like I'd been both shaken *and* stirred.

"Breathe," Gabriel whispered, pushing my hair off of my forehead and handing me a shirt and shorts that he pulled out of God knows where. "You might want to put this on. You've been through quite the ordeal."

At his angelic touch, the madness settled and the room came back into focus. The helpless feeling of not being in control of my own body ebbed. The senselessness of the white experience faded. The horrible and heartless words Anabael used my mouth to say flashed through my mind and burned through my heart.

"Who—where…?" I tried to speak, as I pulled the shirt over my head, but when I did, I could only seem to get one word out at a time, unable to grasp what I wanted to say. Something about the white void and Michael and Raphael came to mind, but I couldn't harness a coherent thought.

"Shhh, it's of no matter right now." As Gabriel's hand passed over my hair, the thoughts and questions floated away like smoke.

Did it even happen? Had it been a dream? Or one final mindfuck from Anabael? I wondered as I slid the soft cotton shorts up to my waist.

As soon as that thought left my head, I questioned what *it* I'd even been thinking about. I felt that maybe some sort of *it* had indeed happened, but I couldn't place a value to *it*.

The more I sat, the more I felt like someone had ripped all my limbs off, beaten me stupid with them, and then stapled them back on wrong.

Twice.

I lifted one arm to poke at the bruised and purple flesh around my wrist. I'd been bound to more than my fair share of tables and gurneys in my day. I knew damn well what the aftereffects looked like. I started to remember…my loved ones, the people in this very room had tied me down. I had been afraid, so very afraid, but on some level I also knew that it had to be done.

"Am I…me?" I asked.

"Very much so," Gabriel said with a smile and a wink.

Glancing to the left, I saw Tess. Josie and Lana had her left arm twisted around her back while Tony and Z had her other wrist pinned to the wall. In her right hand was a long dagger gripped so tightly her knuckles were ghostly white. They all stared, open-mouthed, at me.

When Tess opened her fist and the dagger clattered to the floor, the others let her go. She bent forward and all but crumpled to the floor, covering her face with trembling hands. I wanted to comfort her, but as soon as I'd swung my legs off of the gurney, the room spun again.

Wait.

"Where's Daniel?"

She looked past me, to something behind me and shook her head.

Turning around slowly, I saw Daniel's handler Chris first. He looked like hell, sickly gray like he was looking upon death itself.

The sight of Daniel sprawled on the other bed, Isolde standing still as a statue over his prone body, gripping the paddles of a defibrillator, made my heart sink. Panic rose in my gut, and I scrambled to my feet, falling several times before I reached the side of his bed and clung to the rail for all I was worth. The eerie sound of one long, continuous beep filled my ears.

No. This couldn't be happening. Gabriel would not bring me back to a world without Daniel, would he?

"The two of you are connected in every possible way," Alex explained. "When you stopped breathing, he dropped like a stone. We've been trying to get him back, but…" Alex shook his head. He laid his hands on my shoulders in what I assumed was an effort to comfort me. Like bloody hell.

Shrugging him off and summoning what little strength I had left in my battered and bruised body, I hauled myself up onto the bed. Droplets landed on Daniel's face as I hovered over him; I hadn't even realized I'd been crying. Grabbing his face, I rested my forehead against his.

"Goddamn it, Daniel, you asshole, don't you dare leave me here by myself. You fight." Any other words shriveled up in my throat, and I all could do was kiss his soft lips.

Beep. My head snapped up and I stared at the monitor, waiting for another blip. There just had to be another—

Beep. My hands ran over his face and his shorn head.

Beep. Daniel's chest began to move up and down rhythmically underneath me.

Beep. His beautiful blue eyes fluttered open and met mine, and I felt like I could finally breathe again.

"Are we dead?" he asked in a tight, gravelly voice.

Normally I would have a snarky retort, but right now, after everything we'd been through, I just couldn't think of anything witty.

"It's okay," he said quietly, his arms closing around me. "I'd never leave you babe, ever."

I melted into him, burying my face into his neck. I didn't like other people seeing me cry, but the sobs wracked me so suddenly, I didn't care who else was in the room. I clutched him like the treasure that he was and dissolved into a snot-sobbing mess.

When I was able to gather my sanity, and stopped crying like a girl all over Daniel, Alex cleared everyone except Isolde from the room and broke down the happenings of the last few minutes while Izzy gave both of us a once-over.

Gabriel had been able to extract Anabael from my body, and I think she'd tried to take every single one of my internal organs with her. God, even my spleen hurt. According to Alex, as soon as Anabael's essence had been removed, I died, right there on the table.

It was weird to hear that because of what people say about dying. I had no recollection of anything. No darkness closing in around me, long tunnels lit from within, or angels descending to usher my soul up to the heavens. But, hold on a minute, there *was* something tucked back in the base of my brain. Not so much of a memory but a… feeling? No, *feeling* wasn't the right word either. I racked my mind for any adjective that would describe it, whatever *it* was. The only thing that kept coming back through my thoughts, over and over again, was white. However, it wasn't the color — it was the feeling of white.

Whatever the blue hell *that* meant.

Apparently when I'd bitten the big one, so had Daniel, which sent the room into some sort of a tizzy.

Tess had grabbed Z's dagger and started rambling that she was going into the afterlife to fetch me because I wasn't allowed to die without her, and it took Josie, Lana, Tony, and Z to keep her from it. She may have been a little bit of a thing, but she was freakishly strong.

Alex had started CPR on Daniel while Isolde had gotten the crash cart ready.

And poor Chris had been torn between talking Tess out of her insane plan to storm the netherworld in search of me and his handler bond to Daniel, who hadn't responded to anything Alex or Isolde tried.

That's when I'd woken up to find Gabriel looking down on me, and my own memory could pick up the happenings.

"To say you've both been through bedlam and back again would be a considerable understatement," Alex said as he stood next to Isolde and placed an arm around her shoulders.

"Indeed," Isolde said, "and physically, you are no worse for the wear. However, I cannot in good conscience release either one of you to your hunter duties, considering the maelstrom you've just experienced emotionally. That includes any and all training. I am prescribing at least three days' bed rest, and since your bedroom has been…compromised, for lack of a better word, I've made up the guest room for you. In short, I don't want to see either one of you outside of that room, *at all*, for three full days."

I opened my mouth to protest because even after all the shit I'd just been through, three days out of the field would drive me absolutely bonkers, and I'd be clawing at the walls to be let out in less than twenty-four hours, guaranteed. That is, until the look on Isolde's face registered with me. Her eyes twinkled the way they did when she was up to mischief, and the corner of her mouth twitched up ever so slightly. That naughty little gypsy; she was ordering Daniel and me to lock ourselves in a room for three days.

Slowly working myself upright with stiff muscles, I slid off the bed and wrapped my arms around her neck.

"Thank you," I whispered into her hair. She was probably the only person in existence who knew how much Daniel and I absolutely *needed* this time alone with each other after what we'd been through.

CHAPTER 24
DANIEL

We made our way back to the guest room, our bodies tired and weak from the brouhaha we'd managed to live through. Pushing through the door, we nearly collapsed with exhaustion onto the bed. And there we slept, in what we were wearing.

Pieces of clothing eventually came off, however, as we stirred to adjust position. Some twenty-four hours later, we woke completely stripped naked and wrapped up in each other's arms, the way we always slept.

I could feel her looking at me, so I opened my eyes. She had risen up on one elbow and was peering down at me. The tiny bristles of hair that had already popped up all over my head began to tingle under her gaze. Like she was answering a call to my need to have some kind of physical contact, she ran her hand over my scalp and smiled. I turned onto my side and faced her, closing my eyes at the sensation of her touch. I turned my head into the feeling and hummed at how glorious it felt.

She hadn't said anything yet, and I was man enough to admit that I was more than a little self-conscious about not having any hair.

"I know it looks weird," I said, slipping my hand over hers, "but it'll grow back."

"I'm not going to lie, I loved playing with your hair, but it would take more than a head-shaving to rub the sexy off of you, baby. I'll just have to find something else to grab on to."

Ev slid her hand over the back of my head and let it trail down my spine to grip a healthy portion of my left butt cheek.

"That'll do." I waggled my eyebrows at her and pressed my arousal into her hip, letting her know just how much that would do for me.

Something in her eyes shifted, though, and she pulled away a little bit and took my face in her hands.

"It wasn't true, what she said. What Anabael said about Z and me and all that—"

"Don't." I laid my forehead against hers reassuringly.

"But what she said, about what we did and it being me…it wasn't and we didn't. You stopped her in time, before she…before Z was even…I had no control over what she did to me *or* him. But I was trying to fight her on the inside when she started that. I knew she was trying to drive a wedge between you and me, trying to pick at something that would break us apart. But that's no excuse. I should have been paying attention to what she was doing on the outside. I should have stopped fighting for myself and fought for us and—"

"Shhh…" I silenced her with a soft kiss. The image of her and Z flickered in my head, but I pushed it away. It hadn't been Evie, and it hadn't gone as far as I'd thought. And the fact was, Z was also a victim in all this and would bear his own scars. So I was bound and determined to wash the incident away and replace it with visions of Evie and me instead—there were a hell of a lot more of those to choose from. "I didn't, for one split second, believe a word of what that creature said."

She cocked an eyebrow at me, and I relented. "Okay, in truth, I'm seriously considering scheduling a session with Z in the training room to work that shit out. But I know that none of that came from you. I know you." I let the backs of my fingers trail down her side, and her body shivered in response. "See?" I smiled down at her. "I know what makes you do that." I reached out with my other hand and grazed her inner thigh. I felt her muscles tighten and heard her breath catch in what I knew was anticipation. "And that." I curled her leg around my hip and let my length press against her opening. It was warm and wet and so inviting, but I held back, teasing her with just the tip. "Not to mention I've seen Z in the locker room, and not to brag or anything, but I really don't think I have anything to worry about, do you?"

I slid into her easily, seating myself good and deep. We both sighed with pleasure and her back arched, pulling me even farther in.

The sensation of my body gliding into her was intoxicating. I withdrew almost all the way out and had to grit my teeth as I slowly pushed back in. She wrapped her other leg around my waist, and I found myself gripping her hips as I slid in so far that my pelvic bone rocked against her clitoris. She moaned quietly, lightly biting my earlobe, and I moved that way again, pressing harder, and was rewarded with the tight grip of what I knew was the beginning of her orgasm.

Our bodies slid together, slow and sure, relishing in every tingle, every lick of pleasure coursing through us. Our tattoos illuminated, lighting every corner of the room, pulsing brighter as our lovemaking soared to a level we'd never reached before. The time we'd been apart, the fear of never being together again, and all of the recent events in the infirmary all culminated into an explosion of pleasure and love.

"This is home," I breathed as I felt my own climax tighten my sack, race up my length, and spill into her.

This was where I belonged, right here with Evelyn. I knew, with one hundred percent of my soul. The zero-point-one percent that had questioned my decision to continue with this life vanished. In truth, it had vanished once I'd opened my eyes and seen Evie. My life. My soul. My home.

Following Isolde's orders, we didn't emerge from that room for three days. Not that we didn't try—I mean, a guy can only live on hot sweaty sex for so long before he has to get some actual sustenance in him. But every single time we opened the door to get something to eat, we'd find a tray of food right outside the door. It was the most glorious three days of my life, and I was so ridiculously glad that I was here for it.

We talked about what had happened to us after we'd died. Evie's experience had come back to her to some degree. She remembered being in a white room that wasn't a room. Of course, that made absolutely no sense to either one of us, so we tried not to overthink what didn't seem important. What *was* important were the two men she'd seen, because I had only seen one, Gabriel.

"Who do you think they were?" I asked as I ran a bare foot up her calf.

"I don't know, but I'm pretty sure I talked to them. I think one of them called me feisty."

"You *are* feisty," I teased. Clearly whoever they were knew her and knew her well. I reached around and tickled her side just to hear the sound of her laugh, one of my favorite sounds in the world.

"What about you?" She ran her hands over the regrowth of my hair; after three days, she said it felt like velvet and she couldn't stop touching it. "You could have had a normal life, been a dad." She looked wistful, like she was picturing me with a baby. I could see her holding a little bundle wrapped up in her arms, too — our baby.

"You would have been a great dad," she said quietly, and I knew by the hitch in her voice that she was fighting off tears.

She'd never mentioned wanting kids before — neither had I, now that I thought about it. From the second I'd seen her, I never regretted my decision to become a hunter or give up my ability to have a child. But maybe it was something that she'd always wanted and I'd somehow picked at an old wound.

"Hey," I said, wiping a tear that had spilled out, "you would have made a great mom."

"Pffft." She shook her head and brushed off another escaped tear. "Are you kidding? Have you met me?"

"Yeah, and you would have been great."

"Why didn't you do it? I mean, I never really liked kids, but you wanted that."

"Once, in another life, I wanted that, but there was one problem with me going back, one that I just wasn't okay with on any level."

"What?"

"It wouldn't have been with you. You are the only one I want. Ever."

Her arms coiled around my neck, and she buried her face in the crook of my neck. I loved it when she did that.

"Besides, who else would put up with your belligerent ass?" I reached down to give her delicious backside a pinch.

"Only another belligerent ass." She laughed and bit at my neck, sending us into a wrestling match that would surely have us both panting when it was over.

EPILOGUE
ALEXANDER

Gabriel perched on the side of my desk, staring at me with his fingers steepled underneath his chin.

My team had just been through the most harrowing time of their lives in the past few weeks, especially Evelyn. But that wasn't surprising. What other hunter could have managed to accomplish what she had and still have a shred of sanity left?

The answer was simple: none. This ordeal with Anabael would have mentally crippled or outright killed any other current hunter in the Lebriga Corporation.

I suppose it *had* killed her, if one was speaking technically. To see her lifeless body on that table had speared my heart with pain like I'd never felt. When Daniel had fallen, it had nearly done me in.

I'd lost hunters in the past; it was part of the business and things happened. But these two...no, if I was being honest, it was the entire crew in my care. Every hunter and handler in my home had a special place in my heart. They were my children, *our* children, Isolde's and mine.

"Well?" Gabriel prompted.

Well, indeed. "She is ready," I answered.

Gabriel hummed his agreement and nodded as he stood and strode across my office. "Yes, we know that, but are you?"

I gazed out of my office window, watching my team go about their daily business.

Across the hall, in their shop, I could hear Tessa and Evelyn argue over the correct pronunciation of a spell. The smell of lotus incense floated down the hall and under the door, and I knew that Isolde was working with Maria on how to help Lana rein in her visions. The lights flickered, and I heard Walter's "Sorry" from the technological laboratory. I could hear the dull thud of fists connecting with flesh as Daniel and Zachary sparred next door in the training facility. I knew Anthony, Josephine, and her handler Margaret were out on assignment to rid Pasadena of a particularly nasty infestation of gremlins. And Christopher and Finn, Z's handler, were working together to create a new weapon that would trap a Spectoral spirit and save the host—we could then save the possessed Beautiful Illuminations women, whom we had under lock-and-key in the basement of a Nevada branch safe house.

I'd been at this for over a thousand years, and after such time in service, I was being given a choice. Was I ready for it? Was Isolde? Could I leave my team, my family? I wasn't certain that I knew how to be different than I was at this time, even if I was indeed "ready" for it.

"When must you know?"

As I turned, Gabriel smiled at me. Surely he knew I was biding my time—he had to; he knew all too well the inner workings of my mind. However, he allowed it. He closed his eyes for a moment before he nodded.

"Michael and Raphael are in agreement. It doesn't have to be now, but it must be soon. Think on it, child. Talk to Isolde *and* Evelyn. She is quite perceptive for one so young and stubborn."

She was. I did not doubt that Evelyn had the ability to lead the team, but I truly did not know if she had the desire. I had known I was supposed to lead from the moment I had taken my vow as a hunter. It was in my blood and bones. What if she declined? Could I live knowing that someone else would lead my family and possibly bring it to ruin?

Gabriel walked over to me and placed a large hand on my shoulder. "You've served the cause well for many years, child, and although you don't say it, I know that you grow tired of the evil in this world. However, Ascension is quite a large step. Make sure it is one that you are willing to take."

I *was* tired. God help me, I was.

"I will let you know my decision soon, on my honor."

"Be well," he said before he vanished before my eyes.

ACKNOWLEDGMENTS

I would like to thank Omnific Publishing for taking a chance on this little author. Elizabeth Harper, our fearless leader, who had a vision to make a publishing family and made it a reality. To the spectacular team of editors and artists, Melissa Simmons, Kimberly Blythe, Coreen Montagna, Micha Stone, and Amy Brokaw, you ladies make it appear as if I actually know what I'm doing. Colleen Keough Wagner, you get the crazy bits of my brain and help me wrangle them into decipherable words that other people understand; you are amazeballs to the nth degree. Traci Olsen, Big T, The Pimptastic Pimpmaster of Publicists, you rock! Victoria Michaels, my Yoda and only living soul that sees my work before any other living soul on the planet, thank you for your continuing guidance and words of wisdom; I truly could not do this without you in my corner. My sisters from other misters, Kim, Mindy, and Lecia, we quite literally live in all four corners of the country, but you are my nearest and dearest friends; thank you for always being behind me and supporting my dream. I love you girls so much, and I can't wait until we can get together and cause some trouble. And last, but definitely not least, my fantabulous love monkeys, my beautiful and spectacular readers, thank you for taking the time out of your lives to read my words. There would be no words without people to read them. <3

·

About the Author

Patricia Leever is a wife, stay-at-home mom of four, and owner of one dog and one really old cat. On the average school day she runs about town like a lunatic picking up and dropping off kids and trying to find a moment of quiet to write down a word or two. She's a sci-fi geek that loves to dress up like a zombie and participate in the local zombie march down Main St. and laugh as much as possible; laughter frees the mind and heals the soul.

Live. Breathe. Write.

PatriciaLeever.wordpress.com

New Adult Romance

Three Daves by Nicki Elson
Streamline by Jennifer Lane
The Shades series: *Shades of Atlantis* & *Shades of Avalon* by Carol Oates
The Heart series: *Beside Your Heart, Disclosure of the Heart* & *Forever Your Heart*
by Mary Whitney
Romancing the Bookworm by Kate Evangelista
Flirting with Chaos by Kenya Wright
The Vice, Virtue & Video series: *Revealed, Captured, Desired* & *Devoted*
by Bianca Giovanni
Granton University series: *Loving Lies* by Linda Kage

Paranormal Romance

The Light series: *Seers of Light, Whisper of Light* & *Circle of Light* by Jennifer DeLucy
The Hanaford Park series: *Eve of Samhain* & *Pleasures Untold* by Lisa Sanchez
Immortal Awakening by KC Randall
The Seraphim series: *Crushed Seraphim* & *Bittersweet Seraphim* by Debra Anastasia
The Guardian's Wild Child by Feather Stone
Grave Refrain by Sarah M. Glover
The Divinity series: *Divinity* & *Entity* by Patricia Leever
The Blood Vine series: *Blood Vine, Blood Entangled* & *Blood Reunited*
by Amber Belldene
Divine Temptation by Nicki Elson
The Dead Rapture series: *Love in the Time of the Dead* & *Love at the End of Days* by
Tera Shanley

Romantic Suspense

Whirlwind by Robin DeJarnett
The CONduct series: *With Good Behavior, Bad Behavior* & *On Best Behavior*
by Jennifer Lane
Indivisible by Jessica McQuinn
Between the Lies by Alison Oburia
Blind Man's Bargain by Tracy Winegar

Erotic Romance

The Keyhole series: *Becoming sage* (book 1) by Kasi Alexander
The Keyhole series: *Saving sunni* (book 2) by Kasi & Reggie Alexander
The Winemaker's Dinner: *Appetizers* & *Entrée* by Dr. Ivan Rusilko & Everly Drummond
The Winemaker's Dinner: *Dessert* by Dr. Ivan Rusilko
Client N° 5 by Joy Fulcher

← ⁓→Historical Romance← ⁓→

Cat O' Nine Tails by Patricia Leever
Burning Embers by Hannah Fielding
Seven for a Secret by Rumer Haven

← ⁓→Anthologies← ⁓→

A Valentine Anthology including short stories by
Alice Clayton ("With a Double Oven"),
Jennifer DeLucy ("Magnus of Pfelt, Conquering Viking Lord"),
Nicki Elson ("I Don't Do Valentine's Day"),
Jessica McQuinn ("Better Than One Dead Rose and a Monkey Card"),
Victoria Michaels ("Home to Jackson"), and
Alison Oburia ("The Bridge")

Taking Liberties including an introduction by Tiffany Reisz and short stories by
Mina Vaughn ("John Hancock-Blocked"),
Linda Cunningham ("A Boston Marriage"),
Joy Fulcher ("Tea for Two"),
KC Holly ("The British Are Coming!"),
Kimberly Jensen & Scott Stark ("E. Pluribus Threesome"), and
Vivian Rider ("M'Lady's Secret Service")

← ⁓→Sets← ⁓→

The Heart Series Box Set (*Beside Your Heart, Disclosure of the Heart &
Forever Your Heart*) by Mary Whitney
The CONduct Series Box Set (*With Good Behavior, Bad Behavior &
On Best Behavior*) by Jennifer Lane
The Light Series Box Set (*Seers of Light, Whisper of Light, Circle of Light &
Glimpse of Light*) by Jennifer DeLucy
The Blood Vine Series Box Set (*Blood Vine, Blood Entangled, Blood Reunited &
Blood Eternal*) by Amber Belldene

← ⁓→Singles, Novellas & Special Editions← ⁓→

It's Only Kinky the First Time (A Keyhole series single) by Kasi Alexander
Learning the Ropes (A Keyhole series single) by Kasi & Reggie Alexander
The Winemaker's Dinner: RSVP by Dr. Ivan Rusilko
The Winemaker's Dinner: No Reservations by Everly Drummond
Big Guns by Jessica McQuinn
Concessions by Robin DeJarnett
Starstruck by Lisa Sanchez
New Flame by BJ Thornton

Shackled by Debra Anastasia
Swim Recruit by Jennifer Lane
Sway by Nicki Elson
Full Speed Ahead by Susan Kaye Quinn
The Second Sunrise by Hannah Downing
The Summer Prince by Carol Oates
Whatever it Takes by Sarah M. Glover
Clarity (A *Divinity* prequel single) by Patricia Leever
A Christmas Wish (A *Cocktails & Dreams* single) by Autumn Markus
Late Night with Andres by Debra Anastasia
Poughkeepsie (enhanced iPad app collector's edition) by Debra Anastasia
Poughkeepsie (audio book edition) by Debra Anastasia
Blood Eternal (A Blood Vine series single, epilogue to series) by Amber Belldene
Carnaval de Amor (The Winemaker's Dinner, Spanish edition)
by Dr. Ivan Rusilko & Everly Drummond

coming soon from
OMNIFIC PUBLISHING

Let's Get Physical by Elle Fiore
The WORDS series: *The Truest of Words* (book 3) by Georgina Guthrie
The Poughkeepsie Brotherhood series: *Saving Poughkeepsie* (book 3) by Debra Anastasia
The Hidden Races series: *Incandescent* (book 1) by M.V. Freeman
The Legendary Saga: *Claiming Excalibur* (book 2) by LH Nicole
The Runaway series: *The Runaway Ex* (book 2) by Shani Struthers
The Forever series: *Forever Autumn* (book 1) by Christopher Scott Wagner
Something Wicked by Carol Oates
Going the Distance by Julianna Keyes